What lurks inside?

In the center of the clearing stood an enormous old tree. A lantern hung from one of its gnarled branches. But the light they had seen from a distance wasn't coming from the lantern. It was coming from *inside* the strange, twisted tree—glowing gold light was pouring through the cracks of a tiny door carved into the thick black trunk.

Nina's heart started to race. One horrible thought after another ran through her brain. What if there was someone behind that door—like a maniac, or a murderer?

She wanted to turn and run. But Sammy took a step forward, and Nina froze in her tracks instead.

They both should have run—because lurking behind that door was something far worse than anything Nina could have imagined . . .

Revenge of the Goblins

DEADTIME STORIES™

Revenge of the Goblins

A. G. Cascone

Troll

For little Nina,
who chases all the goblins away.

CHAPTER 1

Nina Michaels didn't hear the footsteps behind her as she wandered deeper into the woods. She was so absorbed in searching the ground ahead of her that she never noticed the horrible creature at her back.

Not until it was too late.

"Don't move," a voice behind her commanded.

Every muscle in Nina's body obeyed. Except for her heart. That muscle started pounding like crazy— especially when she realized what was sliming its way up the back of her neck and wrapping itself around her throat.

"Get it off!" Nina ordered, barely moving her lips. "Get it off me right now!"

Sammy Burke cracked up as he reached out and snatched the snake off Nina's shoulder.

Nina's skin was crawling as she watched the disgusting creature coil itself around Sammy's hand.

"It's just a garter snake." Sammy laughed at her as he waved the snake's creepy little face in front of her nose.

"You're such a jerk!" Nina shrieked, jumping away. "I don't know why I even talk to you sometimes!"

"Because I'm your best friend," Sammy reminded her with a wicked grin.

Sammy was right. He was her best friend. But today he was acting like her worst nightmare. Nina hated it when he played stupid practical jokes on her.

No one could get one over on Nina the way Sammy could. That was because no one in the whole world knew her as well as Sammy did. He knew all the things she liked best, and all the things she hated most. Snakes were definitely at the top of the "hate" list.

"You're so gross," Nina said, watching Sammy play with the snake. "How can you even touch something so smelly and slimy?"

"He's not smelly," Sammy protested. "And he's not slimy either. He feels like leather. Touch him and you'll see. There's nothing to be afraid of." He shoved the snake in her face again.

"Get that thing away from me!" Nina smacked Sammy's arm, and the snake went flying.

"Hey!" Sammy complained. "What's the matter with you?"

"I hate snakes," Nina told him.

"You're just mad because I'm winning," he said.

"I am not," Nina snapped.

"Yes, you are," Sammy needled. "You're mad because you haven't found a single animal yet."

Sammy was right about that too. But Nina wasn't going to admit it. During their hike in the woods, Sammy had spotted a chipmunk, a woodpecker, a baby rabbit, a fat little gopher, and now a disgusting garter snake. The only thing Nina had seen first was a squirrel, and squirrels didn't count—they were everywhere.

"Well, guess what?" Nina shot back. "You win, because I quit."

"Oh, come on," Sammy moaned. "You can't quit. We haven't seen a deer yet."

"I don't want to see a deer," Nina lied. "Besides, it's starting to get dark. If we don't get home, we're going to get in trouble."

"Not until we find a deer," Sammy insisted.

Nina huffed. "If you really want to see a deer, all we have to do is go sit in our own backyards and wait for them to come out of the woods. They come out every night."

"You're no fun," Sammy complained.

Nina just ignored him and started walking.

"You're going the wrong way," Sammy called after her.

"Am not," she said, turning around to see him just standing there. "This is the way home."

Nina and Sammy explored the woods behind their houses nearly every day, venturing deeper and deeper into the forest each time they went. Today, they had gone farther than ever before. But Nina had carefully watched the path they'd taken to make sure they'd find their way out.

Nina scanned the track ahead. *Sammy's just trying to pull another practical joke on me,* she told herself. The sun was starting to go down, and the light creeping through the leafy branches cast eerie shadows on the ground. If Sammy *was* joking, Nina didn't appreciate it.

"It's not the right way," Sammy insisted. "I hate to tell you this, Nina," he went on in a serious tone, "but we're lost!"

A little voice inside Nina's head told her that Sammy was right. But Nina ignored it. It was too scary to think that they might be lost in the woods as night fell. Who knew what kind of creepy things they might spot in the pitch darkness?

Nina took a deep breath to steady her nerves. "This is the way we came," she told Sammy firmly. "If we just follow this route, we'll be back in my yard in no time." Nina started walking again.

The leaves on the ground rustled as Sammy rushed to catch up with her.

"I still think you're wrong," he said. "We came the other way. You got so freaked out by that snake, your sense of direction is all mixed up."

"My sense of direction is never mixed up," Nina protested.

"I'm telling you—" Sammy started to argue again.

But Nina cut him off. "I know where I'm going," she insisted.

Sammy shrugged as he followed. His face kept saying, *"You're wrong,"* while Nina's kept saying, *"Shut up."*

They walked along in silence for a long time. Too long.

Nina was beginning to get nervous. They should have been home by now. But home was nowhere in sight. The woods were getting thicker and darker. She could hear an owl hooting in the distance. Maybe Sammy was right. Maybe they *were* lost.

Nina was about to admit her mistake and suggest that they head back in the other direction when she spotted a clearing up ahead. She could see a faint light shining in the distance.

"I told you I knew where I was going," Nina gloated. She pointed to the light. "That's the light from my back porch!" She raced ahead so fast Sammy had to hurry to keep up.

A second later the little voice inside Nina's head spoke up again. This time it shouted that something was wrong—terribly wrong. The trees that surrounded them were bigger than any of the trees near Nina's backyard. They were twisted, dark towers of black-speckled wood. Their huge, gnarled branches reached downward like long fingers trying to grab her.

Suddenly, the earth beneath Nina's feet felt unfamiliar too. It was muddy and soft, not rocky and hard like the ground near her backyard.

Nina tried desperately to force the warning voice out of her head as she kept moving forward. *This is the right way,* she told herself. *You're almost home.*

By the time they reached the clearing, Nina had managed to convince herself it was true. Once she stepped into the clearing, she would be on her own lawn, looking at her own house, with Sammy's house right next door.

But that wasn't what she saw at all.

Nina stopped walking. Sammy stopped right behind her.

"What the heck is that?" he whispered in a frightened voice.

Nina was too spooked to answer. In the center of the clearing stood an enormous old tree. A lantern hung from one of its gnarled branches. But the light they had seen from a distance wasn't coming from the lantern. It was coming from *inside* the strange, twisted tree— glowing gold light was pouring through the cracks of a tiny door carved into the thick black trunk.

Nina's heart started to race. One horrible thought after another ran through her brain. What if there was someone behind that door—like a maniac, or a murderer?

She wanted to turn and run. But Sammy took a step forward, and Nina froze in her tracks instead.

They both should have run—because lurking behind that door was something far worse than anything Nina could have imagined.

CHAPTER

2

"This is too cool," Sammy said as he started toward the little door.

Cool was definitely not the word Nina would have picked. *Creepy* was more like it. "What are you doing?" she cried as she grabbed Sammy's arm to stop him.

"I want to check it out," Sammy told her. "I've never seen a tree house *inside* a tree before."

Neither had Nina. But she didn't want to see one. At least not one that was standing in the middle of the dark, deserted woods, woods that she didn't even recognize anymore. "How do you know it's a tree house?" she asked nervously.

"It must be," Sammy said. "Why else would there be a door?" Sammy took another step forward.

Nina stopped him again. "I don't think this is such a good idea."

"Why not?" Sammy demanded.

"What if somebody's in there?" Nina asked. "What if he's a maniac or something?"

"Oh, right." Sammy laughed. "Like that could really happen. Maniacs don't live in tree houses."

"How do you know?" Nina shot back. "Maybe it's a murderer who's hiding from the police. Or maybe it's someone who's just waiting for two stupid kids to get lost in the woods so he can jump out of his tree and grab them!"

Sammy smirked. "You watch too many cop shows," he told Nina. "I bet those Shoe-monkey kids did this."

"What Shoe-monkey kids?" Nina asked.

"You know," he said, "Mr. and Mrs. Peerson's grandsons. They were visiting here last summer, remember?"

"Shoe*mocker*," Nina corrected him. "And they were only here for a weekend. There's no way they could have carved out a tree in two days!"

"Then somebody else did it," Sammy said. "I'm just going to peek through the window, okay? If there's a maniac inside, I'll tell you to run."

Nina held her breath as Sammy pressed his nose up against the tiny glass window in the center of the door.

"I can't see anything," he reported a second later. "The window's too grimy."

"Good," Nina declared. "Let's just get out of here."

"Not yet," Sammy said, reaching for the wooden handle on the door.

"Are you out of your mind?" Nina shrieked.

But Sammy ignored her.

Nina felt a chill crawling up her spine as the latch on the door clicked open.

"I told you it wasn't a maniac's house," Sammy gloated. "No way a maniac would leave the door to his tree house unlocked."

Sammy's ridiculous reasoning didn't make Nina feel any better. In fact she was terrified, especially when Sammy crouched down and headed through the door.

"Come on," he said to Nina.

She did *not* want to go inside that tree. But there was no way she was going to stand alone *out*side it either.

Please don't let there be a maniac in there, Nina prayed as she headed for the tree. Then she took a deep breath and ducked through the door.

She felt as if she were Alice stepping through the looking glass. But what was waiting on the other side of the tree house door was even weirder than Wonderland.

Nina couldn't believe her eyes. The inside of the tree was as big as a house—a real house. It was ten times as wide as its trunk!

The hollowed-out wood created a giant circular room. One side of the room was set up like a den, with a sofa shaped like a braided pretzel with squishy green seats. The other side looked like an upside-down kitchen, complete with a potbellied wood-burning stove.

In the center of it all stood a long spiral staircase that led up to nowhere. Next to that was an even longer staircase that led down into the ground, under the roots of the tree.

"Check this out!" Sammy pointed to the lopsided shelves that lined the walls. Each one was loaded with long, skinny test tubes and fat, twisted jars. A bubbling red liquid boiled away in some of the test tubes, while others were filled with smoldering crystals and colored smoke.

"It looks like a mad scientist's lab," Nina said. Several jars contained wormy, peanut-shaped blobs that looked to Nina like brains. Across from the shelves was a long, jagged-edged board lined with dozens of huge eggs wrapped in pulsating purple-blue veins.

But weirdest of all was the neon glow that filled the whole place. Golden, laserlike beams of light penetrated the interior of the tree. Nina froze as she realized they were emanating from a small, shadowy figure in the corner of the room. In his hands was a glowing gold ball.

Nina gasped so loudly, Sammy jumped.

"What?" he cried as he spun around. "What's the matter?"

Nina pointed at the creepy, monsterlike little man.

"It's just a statue." Sammy laughed when he saw the small figure. "It's like a Lava lamp," he said. "Only cooler. Check it out."

Nina didn't want to check *anything* out. But Sammy wasn't about to leave until she did. Nervously she followed him across the carpet of red moss that covered the floor.

Up close, the statue wasn't anywhere near as scary as it was from across the room. In fact, it was kind of silly-looking.

Its bubbly, squished face looked like a Halloween monster mask. Its twisted, clawed feet were twice the size

18

of its short, stumpy legs. Its long, skinny arms were double the length of its body. And its huge, ugly head was way out of proportion with its too-small body.

The only things that didn't look silly were the creature's teeth and its claws. The teeth were a good three inches long, and the sharp, pointed claws were even longer.

"It looks like a little goblin," Nina said as she reached out to touch its cold stone face.

Sammy didn't answer. He was too busy examining the glowing ball it held in its claws. "I wonder how this thing works," he said. "It's not plugged in or anything."

"We're in a tree," Nina pointed out. "There *is* no electricity!"

"Maybe there are batteries in it, or something else that makes it light up." Sammy reached out to pry the luminous orb from the goblin's stone grasp.

"Don't do that!" Nina warned him.

But it was too late. The ball was already in Sammy's hands.

Suddenly, Nina felt the cold, hard statue begin to turn warm and soften under her touch. In fact, it was getting squishy and slimy, and turning a sickly green!

Nina pulled her hand away in a panic. "Sammy, look!" she cried.

Sammy was already looking. "What's going on?" he yelped.

But the answer was obvious.

The creepy green goblin with the long, sharp fangs and pointed claws was coming to life!

CHAPTER

3

Nina was so scared that she felt as if *she* had been turned to stone. Every muscle in her body froze in fear. She tried to scream, but all that came out was a strangled whimper.

She just stood there, staring wide-eyed as the horrible creature opened its mouth and let out a fearsome roar.

"Run!" Sammy cried in a panic as he turned and took off for the door.

But Nina didn't follow. She couldn't. Her feet felt rooted to the floor.

The goblin reached out his long, slimy arms to grab her. His sharp, pointed claws dug into her flesh as they started to close down around her shoulders.

"Sammy!" The scream finally burst free from Nina's throat. "Help me!"

Sammy spun around fast.

"Run, Nina, run!" he yelled as he ripped her away from the creature's clutches and shoved her hard toward the door.

Nina toppled through the little doorway, banging her head on the way out. Sammy was right behind her. He stumbled over her as she fell, face first, onto the ground.

"Get up!" he shouted, pulling her to her feet by the back of her sweatshirt. "We've got to get out of here!"

The goblin burst through the door, growling like a ferocious dog.

Nina and Sammy took off across the clearing and headed for the woods.

The growling green goblin followed right behind them.

"Where are we going?" Nina cried as she and Sammy tore deeper and deeper into the dark woods.

Sammy didn't answer. There wasn't time.

The goblin was gaining on them. Nina could hear his footsteps rustling the leaves behind them.

"He's still chasing us," she screamed to Sammy.

Sammy ran even faster.

Low-hanging branches whipped Nina's face as the path ahead of her narrowed. She kept her head down to protect her eyes, but it was so dark she could barely see the ground below her. Suddenly a twisted vine caught her ankle like a trip wire. Nina's legs buckled. She slammed into the ground, knocking the wind out of her.

The goblin was sure to get her now!

Nina tried to call out to Sammy, but she couldn't get enough air into her lungs.

It was over.

I'm doomed, Nina thought. There's no point in even trying to struggle.

Nina let her whole body go limp on the ground as she started to cry.

"Nina!" Sammy screamed as he realized that she was no longer behind him. He turned around and headed back toward her.

As Sammy drew closer, Nina listened for the goblin. But the only footsteps she could hear were Sammy's.

"What are you doing?" Sammy hollered at her. "Get up!" He reached down to pull her to her feet. "We have to get out of here!"

Sammy started to tug her forward. But Nina tugged back. "Shhhh." Nina gestured for Sammy to be quiet. "Listen," she said. "I don't hear him anymore."

The two of them stood there silently for a minute.

Nina was right. There was no sound in the woods but their own heavy breathing. No crunching leaves. No horrible growls. Just silence.

"What a relief!" Sammy said. "We're safe."

"Not yet we're not," Nina corrected him. "We may have ditched that creepy little creature, but we've still got to find our way home." Nina looked around frantically, trying to spot anything that would give her a clue.

Sammy looked around too, but neither one of them recognized a thing.

"We're never going to find our way out of here," Nina sighed hopelessly.

"We are too." Sammy tried to sound brave.

"Oh, yeah?" Nina challenged him. "How?"

"Maybe if we just pick a path and keep walking straight, we'll find our way to a road," he said. "Then we'll be able to figure out how to get home."

It wasn't much of an idea, but it was all they had. Nina nodded her agreement. "Which way?" she asked.

"Well, we don't want to go back that way." Sammy pointed in the direction from which they'd come. "The last thing we want to do is run into that goblin again."

"Then we'll keep going straight ahead," Nina decided. She figured that was the best way to avoid the little monster.

But she was wrong.

Before they could take even one step, something dropped from the branches overhead onto the path in front of them, blocking their way.

The instant Nina saw what it was, she began to scream.

CHAPTER
4

The growling green beast stood less than two feet in front of Nina and Sammy, glaring at them with his glowing red eyes.

This can't be happening! Nina's brain refused to believe what her eyes could see clearly.

"Where did he come from?" Sammy cried, staring at the goblin, petrified.

The goblin just stared back.

Nobody made a move.

"What are we going to do now?" Nina whispered, barely moving her lips.

As the goblin took a step toward them, the answer became obvious.

"Run!" Sammy turned around and pushed Nina ahead of him. They were running back the way they'd come.

"We shouldn't be going this way," Nina cried. "We'll end up back at his house."

"You're right," Sammy agreed. "Head that way." He pointed off to the left.

A moment later the goblin was in front of them, blocking their way again.

"This way!" Sammy shouted, turning completely around.

Nina followed his lead.

For a minute, it looked like they were safe. But just for a minute.

Sammy stopped short. Nina slammed into him. "What are you doing?" she hollered.

But Sammy didn't answer. He didn't have to.

The goblin was in front of them again. He raised his long, warty arms over his head and let out a horrible growl. Then his green, pointed claws reached out . . . right for their throats!

Without a word, Sammy and Nina took off in yet another direction.

"How does he keep getting in front of us?" Nina shrieked.

"I don't know," Sammy answered. He was panting hard from running.

So was Nina. She didn't know how much more she could take. Her lungs were burning. Her legs ached. And she had a horrible pain in her side.

"Look!" Sammy shouted excitedly, just as Nina was about to collapse. "We're almost home!"

Nina looked up ahead and saw a light. This time, it really was her porch light. Just a few more feet and they would be out of the woods and back in their own backyards.

But the goblin dropped out of nowhere to block their way again.

They couldn't change direction this time. Nina's heart pounded and she could barely breathe. What were they going to do now?

"Bread and butter," Sammy suddenly shouted.

She knew just what he meant.

He ran to the right, she to the left. Before the goblin could decide which one of them to grab first, they'd made it past him.

"All right!" Nina cried. "We did it!" Nina looked back over her shoulder as she made a mad dash for her house. But that was a mistake. She was so happy to see nothing behind her, she missed what was lunging at her from in front.

"Look out!" Sammy shouted.

But it was too late. Before Nina knew what was happening, she was knocked to the ground by a monstrous beast.

"Noooooooo!" Nina cried, swinging her arms wildly to try to escape. It was useless. She was already pinned beneath the creature. Drool rolled off his fangs and dropped on her face. Nina tried to turn away as the creature's wet, squishy nose pressed up against hers. His hot breath swirled its way up her nostrils.

26

He's going to kill me! Nina's voice cried in her head. *Then he'll cut out my brain and put it in one of those jars on his shelf!*

"Get off her!" Sammy shouted.

Nina felt the weight of the creature being tugged from her body. When her eyes finally focused, she saw that her attacker wasn't a goblin at all. It was Huey! Nina had never been so glad to see Sammy's big golden retriever.

"What's the matter with you, you stupid dog?" Sammy scolded him as Nina rose to her feet.

"Don't yell at Huey," Nina scolded Sammy back. "He didn't mean to scare me, did you, boy?"

Huey wagged his huge tail. Then he jumped up on Nina and licked her, *splat*, in the face.

"Okay, okay." Nina giggled, trying to escape Huey's slobbery tongue. The truth was, she didn't care if Huey licked her whole face. She was too relieved that they'd gotten rid of that goblin to worry about dog spit.

"Come on, Huey. Get down." Sammy reached out to grab Huey's collar.

Suddenly, Huey lost all interest in Nina. He stopped wagging his tail and stopped licking her face. His ears went back and his fur stood on end. As he began to snarl, Nina's eyes flicked back toward the woods. Sure enough, the hideous goblin stood there, his beady red eyes burning through the darkness.

"No!" Nina grabbed for Huey's collar, trying to hold him back.

But Huey broke away and charged at the goblin, barking ferociously.

Nina covered her face with her hands. She didn't want to watch what happened next.

But nothing happened. Because the creepy little goblin ran away.

"Way to go, boy!" Sammy congratulated his dog. As Huey bounded back toward them, Sammy patted him on the head. "Can you believe the way he protected us?" he said to Nina.

Nina *couldn't* believe it. She hadn't thought Huey had it in him to be so fierce. She'd always thought of him as just a dopey, lovable old dog.

"Good boy," she said to Huey, rewarding him with a kiss on the top of his head. "You saved us."

"That was a close call," Sammy said as they hurried toward their houses.

"Sure was," Nina agreed, nervously glancing back at the woods. "Do you think that thing really was a goblin?" she wondered aloud. It was just too bizarre to believe.

"Well, it wasn't a giant green chipmunk," Sammy shot back. "And that tree house definitely didn't belong to a squirrel."

"But where did it come from?" Nina asked. "And what was it doing in that tree?"

Sammy shrugged.

"You don't think it'll come out of those woods, do you?" Nina asked.

Sammy shook his head. "I doubt it. At least not with Huey around."

"Yeah, well, I'm never going back into those woods again," Nina stated. "Not with that goblin lurking out there."

"Tell me about it," Sammy agreed. "I'm just glad it's over."

But it wasn't over.

"Uh-oh," Sammy said a second later. He stopped in the middle of the lawn.

"What?" Nina jumped.

"Look what I've still got." He pulled his hand out of his pocket. Lying in his palm was the ball that the goblin had been holding when he was still a statue. As the ball rested in Sammy's hand, it started to glow again.

"What are you doing with that thing?" Nina gasped.

"I must have shoved it in my pocket when that creep started chasing us," Sammy said.

"Oh, great!" Nina huffed. "That's probably *why* he was chasing us. He wants it back!"

"I would have given it back if I'd known I had it," Sammy defended himself. "But it's too late now."

"Let me see it," Nina said, reaching for the ball.

The instant Nina's fingers touched it, they began to tingle. She quickly dropped the ball back into Sammy's hand. "There's something wrong with this thing," she told him. "It's like it's full of electricity or something. Don't you feel it?"

Sammy held the ball out in front of him, keeping his

hand very still. "I do feel something," he admitted. "It's vibrating." He looked at the ball curiously. "What if it's got some kind of powers? I mean, everything in that goblin's tree house was pretty freaky."

Nina didn't even want to think about that possibility. If the ball really did have some kind of powers, the goblin was sure to come for it. And that was the last thing they needed. "What are we going to do with it?" she asked.

"Keep it, I guess," Sammy answered.

"Are you nuts?" Nina shot back. "We can't keep that thing."

"Why not?" Sammy said. "What do you want to do? Bring it back to him?"

That was out of the question. "No way," Nina said.

"Then we'll keep it," Sammy announced.

Nina knew that was their only choice. But as she watched Sammy cram the ball back into his pocket, a little voice inside her head told her that holding on to the ball was going to be a big, big mistake.

CHAPTER **5**

Nina couldn't stop worrying about the goblin even after she and Sammy were safely inside their own houses.

Sammy was convinced that the grotesque creature was gone for good. He was sure that his dog had scared the goblin so badly he would never set foot out of his tree house again, or try to get his ball back.

But Nina wasn't so sure. In fact, she worried herself sick about it all night.

Her parents decided she was "overly exhausted." That's what they always said when they thought she was getting upset over "nonsense." They didn't believe a word of her story about the goblin and his tree house. They just scolded her for being out in the woods in the first place. They sent her to bed right after dinner, insisting she needed "her rest."

But there was no way Nina was going to get any rest—not when the window by her bed faced her very worst nightmare.

Maybe every tree in the woods is full of growling green goblins that rip out your brains and keep them in jars! Nina thought.

As she lay in bed, she kept her head under her pillow so that she wouldn't have to look at the woods, but after a while she needed some air.

Slowly Nina removed the pillow from her head. The wind outside howled as it whipped through the woods. She could see dark, eerie shadows as the leaves on the trees struggled to cling to their branches.

Nina's heart started to pound. Maybe they weren't shadows at all! Maybe they were creeping green goblins!

Suddenly, Nina felt thousands of eyes staring up at her, watching and waiting. She was sure that if she fell asleep, an army of goblins would creep out of the woods and into her room, ready to attack!

Stop it! Nina tried to order the crazy thoughts out of her head. *Just stop it!* There was no way there was an army of goblins in those trees. No way at all. There was only one goblin—one goblin who would never come out of the woods.

Nina buried her face back under her pillow.

But as she did, the sound of the wind started to change. It was no longer howling. Now it was growling—a low, evil growl that sent shivers crawling across Nina's skin.

Nina sprang up and pressed her nose against the glass.

The shadows outside were still shifting. Slowly one of them moved away from the trees . . . onto the lawn . . . and into the bushes behind Sammy's house!

Nina let out a gasp as she watched a squished, ugly head pop out of the shrubs. A long, warty arm pulled back the last little branch that stood in its way. Then a bony, gnarled foot stepped through the bushes.

It *was* a goblin! The same goblin Nina and Sammy had seen before! Nina was sure of it.

Sammy's wrong, Nina thought. *The goblin really does want his ball back, and he's coming to get it!*

Nina knew she had to warn Sammy. But how?

The goblin drew closer and closer to Sammy's house. He bent low to the ground, sniffing around like a bloodhound.

Nina reached for the phone on her nightstand. She hoped that Sammy would answer. There was no way she'd be able to convince his parents that there was a goblin outside their house. Mr. and Mrs. Burke would just hang up on her, after first scolding her for calling so late.

But the phone line was busy.

"Darn it!" Nina slammed down the phone. She was about to dial again when she saw the goblin start to climb up the back of Sammy's house!

Nina watched in horror as the creature swung from the gutter like a monkey, leaping from one window frame to the next until it finally landed outside Sammy's room.

"Noooooo!" Nina cried in a panic. She banged on her window to scare him away.

The goblin's grotesque head turned toward the sound.

Nina jumped back from the window, just as the goblin dropped to the ground.

She hadn't scared him at all.

The goblin wasn't running away. He was running straight for Nina!

CHAPTER 6

Nina tore out of her room in a panic. The goblin would be crashing through her bedroom window any second. She could already hear the thing clawing its way up the drain pipe.

"Mom! Dad!" Nina cried as she burst through their door and ran for their bed. "There's a goblin climbing up the side of our house!"

Nina's mom let out a moan as she propped herself up on her pillow. Her dad didn't budge. He just lay there on his stomach with his head buried under the blankets.

"What's climbing up the house?" her mother asked, still half asleep.

"The goblin!" Nina told her. "The one from the woods!"

Mrs. Michaels rolled her tired eyes. "You were just having a bad dream," she said. "Go back to bed."

"No, I wasn't!" Nina insisted. "That goblin is after me!

Daddy, wake up!" Nina shouted at him, tugging at his arm. "You have to do something!"

Nina's father finally rolled over and looked up.

"The goblin's outside our house," her mother informed him, sounding somewhat amused.

"I heard," Mr. Michaels mumbled.

"He is!" Nina shouted. "And if you don't do something fast, he's going to be *inside* our house instead!"

"Nina." Mr. Michaels sat up. "Calm down, sweetheart. There is no such thing as a goblin."

"There is too!" Nina shouted, tugging her father to his feet. "There's one trying to break into my room! I heard him climbing up the drain pipe!"

Nina's mother chuckled as Nina started pulling her father toward the door.

"Be right back," he said, winking at Mrs. Michaels.

"Hurry," Nina said, dragging her father by the hand toward her room.

The instant they reached the doorway, Nina stopped dead in her tracks. "You go first," she told her father. She scrambled to get behind him.

"You really are scared, aren't you?" her father asked.

"Yes," Nina shot back. "And you will be, too, when you see that creepy green creature swinging outside my window like a monkey!"

"I thought he was goblin," her father teased her.

"Just go," she ordered, shoving him through the doorway. She clung to the back of his pajama shirt as he stepped into the room.

Nina flicked on the lights and swept her eyes around the room. "Oh, good," she sighed with relief. "He hasn't gotten in yet."

Her father shot her a smile as he headed for the window and looked out.

Nina held her breath.

"There's nothing out here," Mr. Michaels announced a second later. "Nothing at all."

"Are you sure?" Nina asked.

"Of course I'm sure," he answered.

"Maybe he's hanging from the roof, or someplace where you can't see him," Nina suggested nervously.

Her father chuckled. "There's nothing on the roof, honey."

Just then, the wind hit the side of the house hard. The shutters outside started to rattle.

Nina let out a scream.

"It's just the wind," her father said. "That's probably what you heard before," he added.

"It is not," Nina said. "I saw him, Dad. He was trying to get into Sammy's house!"

"I thought he was trying to get into our house," her father said. "Look, Nina, you just had a bad dream."

Nina knew there was no point in trying to explain any further. Unless her father saw the goblin for himself, he was never going to believe her. Wordlessly, she let him tuck her into bed.

"Now what do you say we try to get some sleep?" he said, giving her a hug. "I'll be right down the hall if you need me."

Nina watched her father head for the door.

"You want me to leave the light on?" he asked.

Nina shook her head. She didn't want her father to think she was a baby. Besides, she could always turn it on again after he left.

"Okay, then," he said. "I'll see you in the morning."

The second her father flicked off the lights, a horrible sound screamed through the window.

Nina jumped.

So did her father.

"What is that?" Nina yelped. Then she realized just what it was.

So did her father. "Aw, geez," he groaned. "Your buddy's security system is going off again."

"It's the goblin!" Nina cried. "I told you he was trying to break into Sammy's house too!"

"It's not the goblin," her father said, heading back to the window. "I'll bet it's Huey. That dumb dog is always setting off the Burkes' alarm." He peered through the window. "You see," he said, pointing to Sammy's yard. "There he is, scratching at their back door."

Nina looked out. Her father was right. Huey really was outside.

The Burkes' alarm stopped screaming as the light on their back porch went on.

"Maybe one of these days they'll build that stupid retriever a dog door so he doesn't wake up the whole neighborhood when he wants to get in," Nina's father said. Then he kissed Nina on the forehead and headed for the door. "Good night, sweetheart," he told her. "Have sweet dreams this time."

Nina stared out the window as Huey started to bark.

He wasn't barking at the back door. He was barking at the woods. Nina could see a shadowy figure cowering behind the trees. Huey could see it too. The dog was baring his teeth, prepared to attack.

Nina swallowed hard. For now, Huey had driven the goblin back into the woods. But Nina knew he'd be back.

CHAPTER 7

Nina sat for hours with her nose pressed up against the window, watching for signs of the goblin. But she didn't see him again.

Still, she kept watching.

The sound of an alarm echoed through the darkness. It sounded so far away that at first Nina didn't think anything of it—until something grabbed her shoulder.

The alarm got louder. Now Nina knew what it was. It was the alarm at Sammy's house. The goblin must have come back! He must have gotten Sammy! And now he had her too!

"Nina!" an agitated voice cried out as the goblin tried to rip her from her bed. *"Wake up!"*

Nina couldn't believe that she'd fallen asleep. She should have been watching. Now the goblin had her, and she was so tired she couldn't make herself fight back. She couldn't even open her eyes. They were so heavy they felt glued shut.

Maybe it was better that way. Maybe it would be over fast and Nina wouldn't have to see a thing.

"Ni-na!" the voice cried again. "If you don't get out of that bed, you're going to be in some serious trouble."

"Nooooooo!" Nina screamed. "Don't kill me!"

This time she forced her eyes open. She blinked hard when she saw the image that loomed over her.

"Then get up," her mother shot back. "Because if you miss that school bus again, I will."

Nina heaved a sigh of relief. She wasn't facing a growling goblin. She was facing a growling mother.

"Didn't you hear your alarm clock?" Mrs. Michaels asked as she pushed the button to turn it off.

Nina shook her head.

"Well, hurry up," her mother said as she headed for the door. "Your breakfast is already on the table."

Nina quickly washed, dressed, grabbed her backpack, and ran down the stairs. She wolfed down her waffles in two seconds flat, kissed her mom good-bye, and tore out the door.

It was 7:38. She had less than three minutes to get to the end of the block and hop on the bus.

Nina started to run.

"Nina!" a voice called from behind her. "Wait up!"

Nina glanced over her shoulder to see Sammy racing after her.

He looked just as harried as Nina. His hair was messy and his shirt was untucked. The laces in his sneakers weren't even tied. But that was the way Sammy looked every morning. Sammy was always late. It was just that this morning, he was even more late than usual.

Nina slowed her pace a little so that Sammy could catch up. "Did you see the goblin last night?" she asked him.

"You mean after you went home?" he puffed as he ran along beside her.

"He was trying to break into your house!" Nina told him.

"What are you talking about?" Sammy asked.

"Didn't you hear your security alarm? Who do you think set it off?" she said.

"That wasn't the goblin," Sammy told her. "That was Huey. He's always setting off the alarm. You know that."

"Huey didn't do it last night," Nina shot back. "The goblin did!"

"Yeah, right." Sammy laughed.

"I'm telling you," Nina insisted. "I saw him! He was hanging on the ledge right outside your window!"

"Was not," Sammy argued.

"Was too!" Nina told him. "And when I banged on my window, he came to my house! But I went and got my parents and then Huey scared him away. He'll be back though. I know it. I'm telling you, that creepy thing wants his ball back. And we'd better give it to him."

"No way," Sammy said as he reached into his

knapsack and pulled out the ball. It was glowing brightly. "This thing is too cool."

Nina couldn't believe him. "Why are you carrying it around with you?" she demanded.

"I'm bringing it to school," Sammy told her. "We can show everybody and tell them what happened yesterday."

"What are you going to tell them?" Nina asked. "That you stole it from a goblin who lives in a tree? Like they're really going to believe that!"

"Good point," Sammy said. "They'll think I'm nuts, huh?"

"Yeah," Nina shot back. "And so do I. You can't bring that ball to school," she went on. "What if something terrible happens? What if the goblin follows you?"

"Well, then I guess everyone *will* believe me," Sammy pointed out.

Nina rolled her eyes. "Just get rid of that thing!" she insisted.

"What do you want me to do with it?" Sammy asked.

Nina didn't have an answer. And she didn't have time to come up with one either. The bus had already stopped at the end of the block. And everybody else was already on it. "Wait!" Nina screamed.

But the bus started pulling away from the curb.

"My mother's going to kill me if she has to drive us to school again!" Nina moaned.

Sammy ran past her, waving his free hand in the air to get the driver's attention.

Nina knew it wouldn't work. Old Mr. Needlemeyer, their bus driver, could barely see three feet *ahead* of him. There was no way in the world he was going to look back.

"Darn it!" Sammy cried as the bus turned the corner, picking up speed.

Nina stopped running. It was hopeless.

"Stop!" Sammy yelled, refusing to give up.

Suddenly, the ball in his hand started to hum. Gold neon beams started shooting out of it like a light show at a rock concert.

Nina's heart came to a complete stop.

So did the bus.

It didn't slow down first, or put on its flashing lights. It just froze right where it was, in the middle of the road.

Something was wrong. Not only had the school bus stopped—so had everybody inside it. All of the kids, and Mr. Needlemeyer, were sitting there, frozen, like statues.

CHAPTER

8

"Cooooooooool!" Sammy exclaimed as he ran toward the bus. "Check it out!"

Nina followed more slowly. Was it her imagination, or had Sammy made that bus stop in its tracks?

Sammy held out the glowing, humming ball. "I told you," he said excitedly. "This thing *does* have special powers."

It had to be true. There was no other explanation for what had happened.

"How does it work?" Nina asked.

"Beats me." Sammy shrugged. "All I did was say 'stop,' and everything stopped. This is terrific!" He pushed open the door of the bus and stepped inside.

"This is terrible," Nina corrected him as she climbed onto the bus behind him.

Mr. Needlemeyer sat motionless.

Nina couldn't resist the urge to reach out and touch him, to see if he felt like a person or like a statue. "Mr. Needlemeyer," she said, poking at his bony old arm. "Wake up!"

He felt perfectly normal. But he didn't wake up.

Nina looked at the passengers. They remained frozen. Their eyes were wide open, but there seemed to be no life behind them.

"Do something, Sammy," Nina insisted. "Start them back up again!"

"I will," he assured her. "In a minute." He walked slowly down the aisle toward the back of the bus, checking out all of their frozen friends. "I want to have some fun first."

"Are you nuts?" Nina shrieked. "What if they all end up stuck like this?"

"Calm down," Sammy told her. "If this ball can stop time, it's got to be able to start it back up again too."

"So do it!" Nina said.

"I want to do something else first." Sammy smiled devilishly.

"Sammy, this is no time for one of your dumb practical jokes," Nina said impatiently.

"You'll like this one," Sammy promised as he continued walking to the back of the bus. "Wouldn't you like to get a good seat?" he asked. "Just for once, wouldn't you like to get the *best* seat on the bus?"

Nina knew just what he meant. "The backseat?" she asked.

Sammy looked over his shoulder and smiled at her. "That's right," he said. "Today you and I are going to sit in the very last seat."

"But Tony Caputo is already sitting in it," she pointed out.

Tony Caputo was the first one on the bus in the morning. He grabbed the backseat every single day, and he refused to let anyone else sit with him. Not that anybody would want to sit next to Tony Caputo. He was the worst bully in the whole school.

"Let's move him," Sammy suggested.

"We can't," Nina said.

"Come on," Sammy urged. "It'll be funny."

Most of the time, Sammy's practical jokes were stupid. But this was one even Nina liked. She put down her backpack and headed to the back to help Sammy. "Where should we put him?" she asked.

Sammy picked the worst possible place. "In the front seat," he told Nina. "Right behind Mr. Needlemeyer."

Nobody ever sat in that seat.

"That's too mean." Nina laughed as she helped Sammy pick up Tony Caputo.

Tony was frozen solid. His right arm was up over his head. In his hand was a paper airplane that he'd been just about to launch.

Nina and Sammy lugged him all the way to the front of the bus and arranged him in his new seat.

"Are you happy now?" Nina asked as she followed Sammy to the back of the bus.

"Very," he answered, flopping into the seat. "How about you?"

Nina nodded as she slid in beside him. "Now please put everything back to normal."

"Okay," he said, taking the ball in both hands. "Here goes. I guess I should just say . . . *Start!*"

The minute the word was out of his mouth, the ball started to hum loudly again. The bus exploded into the noisy zoo it usually was.

Nina looked at the kids around them. They were acting as though nothing had happened.

Except Tony Caputo.

"What do you think you're doing, you little hooligan?" Mr. Needlemeyer hollered at Tony.

Tony had thrown his paper airplane, and it had hit Mr. Needlemeyer right in the back of the head.

"I'm going to tell the principal that you do nothing but cause trouble on this bus," Mr. Needlemeyer ranted on.

Usually when Mr. Needlemeyer hollered at Tony, Tony had something smart to say back. But not this time. This time Tony was too shocked to speak. He just sat there, looking around with a stupid, confused expression on his face.

Sammy put his head down to hide his laughter. "This is great!" he whispered to Nina.

Nina couldn't help chuckling too.

"I'm going to stop time again," Sammy snickered. "Then we can move Tony someplace else and really mess him up."

Nina didn't think that was such a good idea. But before she could say anything to stop him, the bus jerked to a halt.

This time it was different. No one was frozen, and the bus was still noisy, even noisier than before. It took Nina a second to realize it wasn't Sammy who'd stopped the bus. It was Mr. Needlemeyer.

"What in blazes is that?" Mr. Needlemeyer hollered. "Something just jumped right in front of this bus. I hope I didn't hit it."

He opened the doors and got out of his seat to go look.

As Mr. Needlemeyer stepped off, something did hit the bus. But not in the front. It hit the back window, hard.

Startled, Nina turned toward the sound, hoping she wouldn't see a smushed squirrel, or even worse, somebody's pet. Unfortunately, it was something much more disturbing than that.

CHAPTER 9

"Sammy!" As she stared at the terrible sight, Nina started hitting Sammy on the arm.

"What's the matter with you?" Sammy said, giving her a shove to stop her.

She pointed frantically toward the back window of the bus.

Sammy looked at her as if she were nuts.

"Look!" she commanded.

He leaned over her and looked. Then he sat back. "What?" he said.

"Don't you see it?" Nina asked.

He looked around her again. "See what?" he asked.

"The goblin!" Nina told him. She tried to keep her voice down so that everyone else on the bus wouldn't hear her.

"Goblin?" Sammy laughed. But he looked anyway.

It was too late. The goblin was gone.

"Nothing out there," Mr. Needlemeyer announced as he got back on the bus and started it up again.

"I'm telling you, it was the goblin!" Nina insisted to Sammy.

"No way!" Sammy shook his head. "I think your imagination is playing tricks on you."

It wasn't her imagination. "I know what I saw," she told Sammy stubbornly. "It was the goblin. I told you he'd come after us for that stupid ball. That thing is nothing but trouble."

"This ball is the coolest thing in the universe," Sammy shot back, tossing it up into the air and catching it. "I'm keeping it. I don't care what you say."

There was nothing for Nina to say, at least nothing that wouldn't land them in a fight. Nina was in no mood for that. So they rode the last few blocks to school in silence.

Mr. Needlemeyer stopped the bus in front of the school building and threw open the doors. The kids poured out. All except Tony Caputo. Mr. Needlemeyer held him back so that they could visit the principal together. Nina heard Sammy snicker as he walked past Tony.

But Nina didn't think their little prank was so funny anymore. Not when there was a horrible goblin with long teeth and sharp claws pursuing them. As she stepped off the bus, Nina took a good look around. She wanted to be sure that the creepy little creature wasn't nearby.

It looked like the coast was clear, but Nina didn't relax until she was inside the building.

Unfortunately, she didn't stay relaxed for very long.

As Nina walked into her classroom, she was stopped dead in her tracks by something truly horrifying.

CHAPTER

10

Nina let out a sound as if she'd been punched in the stomach. "I can't believe this," she groaned.

Sammy was right behind her. "What a nightmare," he whispered.

Written on the chalkboard in big, block letters were the worst words in the world: **POP QUIZ!**

Nina trudged to her seat. Math was the first subject of the day. It was also Nina's worst subject. She rarely got better than a *C* even when she'd studied for hours. Pop quizzes were always a disaster.

Nina fell into her chair just as the bell rang. She grabbed her math book and started flipping pages frantically. She didn't even know what she was looking for. She just hoped to spot something that would help on the quiz.

Mrs. Flatly, their teacher, headed over to close the door to the classroom.

Tony Caputo slipped through at the very last second.

"You're late," Mrs. Flatly scolded.

"Sorry," Tony said, not sounding the least bit sorry. He didn't bother explaining that the reason he was late was because he'd been to the principal's office, even before the school day began.

Tony took his seat as Mrs. Flatly passed out the quizzes.

A quick look at the problems on the paper told Nina she was doomed. She glanced over at Sammy, expecting his expression to be as pained as her own. But it wasn't. Instead Sammy was smiling.

Nina furrowed her brow, wondering what Sammy was up to.

He winked as he showed her the answer. It was in his hand—the goblin's ball.

Nina shook her head no.

"Okay, class," Mrs. Flatly called for attention. "You have fifteen minutes to complete this quiz. When the time is up, I will say 'stop.'"

But Sammy beat her to it. "Stop!" he commanded.

Everybody did. Everybody but Sammy and Nina.

As Nina looked around the room, she wondered why she was still moving. After all, Sammy was holding the ball. Maybe it was because she was with Sammy when he took it. Or maybe it was because she'd touched the ball, too, the day before. Whatever the reason, Nina was grateful that she *wasn't* frozen like everyone else around her.

Miserable expressions were plastered on all the kids' faces while their hands, which had been reaching for pencils, were stopped in midair. Mrs. Flatly was in the process of sitting down, but she hadn't quite made it all the way to her chair. Now her body was stuck in that position.

Nina might have laughed if she hadn't been so horrified. "What do you think you're doing?" she shrieked at Sammy.

"I'm fixing it so that you and I get an *A* on this quiz," he answered. Then he got up and went to Mrs. Flatly's desk. "She always keeps the answers in front of her." He swiped the paper off the desk and brought it back to his own.

"I can't believe you're doing this," Nina gasped as she watched Sammy copy the answers.

"It beats failing," he told her. "Besides, no one will ever know."

"*I'll* know," Nina said.

"So what are you going to do?" Sammy asked without even looking up from his work. "Tell on me?"

"No," Nina admitted grudgingly.

"And I won't tell on you either," he said, holding out Mrs. Flatly's page with the answers.

"I can't." Nina shook her head.

"Would you rather fail?"

Nina thought about it. It sure would be nice to get an *A*

in math just once. Nobody would ever know what she'd done. And it wasn't as if she were hurting anyone . . .

She hated herself for doing it, but she snatched the paper out of Sammy's hand.

Sammy watched as she began filling in answers. Then he got up and headed to the front of the classroom again.

"What are you doing now?" Nina asked nervously.

"You just finish the quiz," he told her.

She could hear him writing on the blackboard as she kept working. They both finished at the same time.

"Sam-my!" Nina hollered when she looked up and saw what he had done.

Sammy stood back from the board admiring his work.

He'd erased the words "pop quiz" and written something else in their place. Now the message on the blackboard read, "Mrs. Flatly has a big butt!"

"You're going to be in so much trouble if you don't erase that," Nina said.

"Not me." Sammy smiled. Then he took the chalk over to Tony Caputo and put it in his hand.

Nina couldn't help laughing. "That's terrible," she said.

But Sammy had something even worse in store for Tony. He took the answer page from Nina and put it on Tony's desk.

That was going too far.

Before Nina could say so, Sammy slid into his own chair, picked up the goblin's ball, and said, "Start!"

The classroom came back to life.

It took less than a second for all the kids to read the words on the board. Soon there were only two people in the room who weren't laughing, Nina—and Mrs. Flatly.

Nina watched wide-eyed as Mrs. Flatly turned toward the blackboard to find out what was so funny. When she turned back to the class, she looked just like Dr. Jekyll must have looked after he turned into Mr. Hyde. Her eyes were narrow little slits, and her mouth was twisted into a terrible grimace.

"Tony Caputo!" Mrs. Flatly growled as she stalked toward him. "You are in big trouble, mister."

"B-but I didn't do it," Tony stuttered, staring dumbly at the piece of chalk that was in his hand.

Then Mrs. Flatly saw the answers to the quiz sitting on Tony's desk.

"What is this?" she shrieked, reaching down to pick up the paper. She studied it for a second, then lifted Tony from his seat by his ear. "That's it, buddy. You and I are going to the principal's office," she snarled. "The rest of you get to work on the quiz," she told the class.

"Somebody set me up," Tony protested as Mrs. Flatly led him away.

Everybody's head was bent over the desk, working on the quiz. Sammy busily pretended to be working on it too.

But Nina's eyes wandered around the room. As she stared out the window, she felt more and more uneasy about what she'd done. She'd never cheated before. Maybe she should just . . .

Suddenly something scrambled across the grass in the playground and disappeared into the bushes. Nina's heart stopped. She'd only caught a glimpse of it out of the corner of her eye, but that glimpse told her exactly what it was—the goblin!

Just then, something skittered across the ground right in front of the window. It went around the corner of the building and was gone.

Another goblin?

No, Nina told herself as her heart started beating again. *It couldn't be. There's only one goblin.*

But as Nina sat there staring out the window, another green creature sprang from the ground like a rabbit emerging from its hole. Within seconds it disappeared into the bushes, just as the first goblin had done.

Nina's stomach tied itself into thousands of tiny knots. She tried to get Sammy's attention, but before she could, Mrs. Flatly stepped back into the room.

Nina watched in horror as another green goblin leaped from the earth and darted across the grass.

"Ms. Michaels." Mrs. Flatly's voice snapped Nina's thoughts back to the classroom. "You're not going to find the answers to this quiz outside that window, young lady. So put those roaming eyes back on your paper."

Nina quickly did as she was told, shooting Sammy a look as she pretended to fill in the answers on the quiz. But the only question Nina was frantically trying to solve was what to do about the goblins—before the goblins figured out what to do about them.

CHAPTER 11

"No way!" Sammy told Nina as they headed out of the school building at the end of the day. "I am not going to give up this ball." He held his knapsack protectively.

Sammy refused to believe that Nina had seen goblins popping out of the earth in the playground. He refused to believe that the goblins were after them. And he refused to believe that there was anything dangerous about keeping the goblin's ball. To him, it was all fun and games.

But Nina knew there was more to it than that. A lot more.

"We have to get rid of that ball," she insisted. "We have to put it back where we found it. Maybe then all the goblins will just go away."

"Forget it!" Sammy shook his head. "I'm having too much fun with this thing."

Just then they passed by the principal's window.

"Check it out." Sammy laughed.

There was Tony Caputo, still sitting in the principal's office, squirming in the hot seat while he listened to yet another lecture.

Thanks to Sammy, Tony had been out of the classroom all day. And because of that, Mrs. Flatly's mood had been much better than usual. She was in such a good mood that she'd let the class out ten minutes early for the school buses.

"If the other kids in our class knew what I did, they'd probably give me a medal," Sammy said. "Too bad I can't tell them. But there's no way I'm sharing this power with anybody else. It's too cool to share."

Nina sighed. Sammy just didn't get it. The ball was fun, but it was also dangerous. Every time Nina thought about the goblins' beady red eyes and sharp, long claws, she got the creeps all over again. Who knew what would happen if they didn't return the ball? Maybe one of the goblins would come back tonight, or maybe *all* of them would!

She was about to tell Sammy this all over again when he gasped loudly.

"Oh, no," he said. "Look at that!"

Nina jumped, expecting to see another goblin springing up from the ground.

But it wasn't a goblin at all. It was just Sammy's mother.

"Sammy! Nina!" Mrs. Burke called to them as she stepped out of her car.

"What's she doing here?" Sammy cringed. There was nothing more geeky than having your mom make a scene in front of other kids.

She kept calling and waving to them as if they didn't see her, as if everybody in the whole world didn't see her.

"Stop!" Sammy said reaching inside his knapsack to touch the ball. "Stop!"

And everything did.

"What do you think you're doing now?" Nina asked, not really wanting to find out.

"Just follow me," Sammy told her.

He led her to his mother's car and opened the back door. "Get in."

Nina did as she was told. Sammy slid in beside her and closed the door. He reached into his knapsack. "Start!" he said.

"Sammy! Nina!" his mother called, still looking toward the school building.

"Mom!" Sammy stopped her. "Over here."

Mrs. Burke spun around and looked in the backseat of the car. Her mouth dropped open, but she didn't say a thing. She just stood there staring at them as if they were Martians.

"Let's go, huh?" Sammy said impatiently.

His mom looked back toward the school, looked at them, and shook her head.

Nina knew that poor Mrs. Burke thought she was losing her mind.

"That was so mean," she whispered to Sammy as his mother got in the car.

Sammy winked at her. "It's better than letting everyone see her picking us up."

Nina couldn't argue with that.

It took Mrs. Burke a minute to get over her shock and find her voice. "I was headed out to the mall, and I thought I'd pick up the two of you on my way and bring you along with me. Your mother said that was fine with her. Unless you'd rather take the bus home," she said to Nina.

"No," Nina answered. "I'd much rather go to the mall."

"Can we have quarters for the arcade?" Sammy asked.

"Sorry," his mother said as she put the car in gear and pulled away from the curb. "No arcade today. I don't have time. I just have to go to the housewares store to exchange something, and then we're out of there."

"Oh, I don't think so," Sammy whispered to Nina as he patted his knapsack.

Nina knew exactly what he was planning to do. And she didn't like it.

CHAPTER 12

Nina scrambled to keep up with Sammy as he followed his mother toward the swinging glass doors in the front of the mall.

"Sammy," she hissed. "Get back here."

Sammy turned around and shot her a wicked grin as he pulled open the door for his mom.

"Hey!" Nina yanked on the back of his shirt as they headed inside. "Will you slow down and listen to me?"

"What?" he huffed.

"You can't do this," Nina insisted. "You can't just stop the whole mall. Who knows what will happen!"

"I do," Sammy shot back. "We'll get to go to the arcade. And my mom won't even know."

"Yeah," Nina said. "And what about the goblins? Huh? What if they followed us here?"

"Nobody followed us," Sammy said, rolling his eyes. "Besides, if any of those little slimeballs show up, we'll just call the cops. Don't worry about it. It's not a problem."

"Come on, you two," Sammy's mother called over her shoulder as she headed for the escalator. "Get a move on."

"Don't do it!" Nina cried as they stepped onto the escalator behind Sammy's mother. "Please!"

Sammy reached into his knapsack anyway.

Nina tried to grab it from him.

"Cut it out!" Sammy shouted in a whisper as he struggled to pull it back.

"No!" Nina whispered even louder. "Give it to me!"

Sammy's mother turned around and shot them a disapproving look. "What in the world are you two fighting about?" she asked.

Nina smiled sheepishly at Sammy's mother.

"Nothing, Mom," Sammy lied. "We're just goofing around."

Nina wanted to tell Mrs. Burke exactly what they were fighting about. But Sammy glared at her as if to say that she'd better shut up.

As soon as Mrs. Burke turned away, Sammy started tugging on the knapsack again.

Nina reached into the bag to grab the ball before Sammy could get his hands on it.

"Stop!" she shouted at Sammy as her fingers touched the metal.

Sammy's knapsack began to glow like a lamp as golden beams of light shot out of it.

Nina pulled her hand out of the bag fast. The ball started to hum loudly.

But everything else in the mall got quiet. The music stopped playing midsong. Loud, harried shoppers stopped gabbing midsentence. There were no sounds at all. No feet shuffling, no bags rustling, no babies crying in their strollers. Everything was suddenly silent.

Nina's heart skipped a beat. She couldn't believe what she had just done. She'd been screaming at Sammy, not at the stupid ball! But the stupid ball had stopped the mall anyway!

Mrs. Burke stood on the escalator like a statue. Even the giant water fountain had stopped squirting its water midstream.

Sammy cracked up. "This is too cool," he said. "And now you can't even blame me!"

"Shut up," Nina grumbled.

"I can't believe you did that." Sammy kept laughing.

"How come this stupid thing doesn't work on *us*?" Nina asked.

"Who knows," Sammy said. "But it's great, isn't it? Look at this. We've got the whole mall to ourselves!"

"Not for long," Nina told him, reaching for the bag.

"What are you doing?" Sammy asked.

"I'm going to start this place up again," she replied.

"Oh, no, you're not," Sammy said, pulling the knapsack away fast. Then he ran up the escalator steps, right past his frozen mother, who stood there clutching the spatula she wanted to return. "We'll be in the arcade, okay, Mom?"

Like his mother was really going to answer.

Nina stood frozen for a second too. She couldn't believe how crazy Sammy was acting.

"Nina," he shouted over the balcony. "Come on! Let's have some fun!" He took off past the escalator and disappeared down the corridor.

"Wait up!" Nina cried as she tore up the steps. No way was she going to stand there alone.

Nina could hear her own footsteps echoing through the mall as she tried to spot Sammy. Every few feet, she stopped to make sure that she couldn't hear any other footsteps sneaking up behind her—namely, goblin footsteps. With everything inside the mall frozen, she couldn't help being spooked. And she couldn't help thinking that the goblins would find them.

"Sammy?" she called out as she headed for the arcade. Sammy didn't answer.

Nina was starting to get nervous. *Maybe the goblins really had followed them to the mall. Maybe they'd already grabbed Sammy!*

As Nina started to walk past the toy store, something jumped in front of her.

"Take that!" the creature growled. He stuck a huge yellow sword in her face.

Nina screamed at the top of her lungs. The sound echoed off the walls of the silent mall, frightening her even more.

"Knock it off," the thing screamed back at her. Nina gasped. It was Sammy, dressed up in shiny plastic armor

66

and swatting at her with a stupid toy sword.

"You scared me half to death!" Nina yelled as she swatted him back with her fists.

Sammy laughed. "Come on," he said, dragging her into the toy store. "Let's play!"

"No way," Nina refused. "We'll get in trouble!"

"Oh, right." Sammy laughed. "Do you think they're going to kick us out or something?" He gestured toward the frozen employees. "We can do whatever we want, and nobody is going to bother us."

Sammy had a point.

"Come on," he said. "It'll be fun!"

Nina thought about it for a second. She had always dreamed about having a whole toy store to herself. And now that she had one, she couldn't say no.

"Okay." She gave in. "But only for a little while."

"Yes!" Sammy exclaimed triumphantly.

The two of them played with everything from toy electric guitars to state-of-the-art computer games, cruising around the store in go-carts. When they were done playing with the toys, they took off to explore the rest of the mall.

They went to the arcade, playing game after game with tokens from the frozen attendant's belt.

They stopped at the Ice Cream Palace and made themselves cones. Working the ice-cream machine was a blast! Nina's cone was a foot tall, half chocolate and half vanilla with rainbow sprinkles.

They went to the computer store. And then the pet

store. Nina was hoping to cuddle the kittens, and Sammy wanted to play with the snakes. But every creature in the place was frozen. It looked more like a stuffed animal store than a pet shop. So Nina and Sammy headed for the sports store instead, where they borrowed bikes to ride around the mall.

Nina was having the time of her life. She'd even managed to stop thinking about the goblin's ball. She was too busy having fun. It felt like she and Sammy owned the whole mall.

But they didn't. In fact, they were sharing it. And they were about to find out with whom. . . .

CHAPTER 13

"This is stupid," Sammy complained as Nina dragged him through the clothes section in Willaby's Department Store. "I don't want to try on clothes."

"Well, I do!" Nina said as she headed for the dressing room.

"I thought you said your mom was going to buy you this outfit for your birthday, anyway," Sammy groaned.

"She is," Nina told him.

"Then why do you have to try it on now?" he asked.

"To see if I really like it," she said. Then she stepped into the dressing room and closed the door behind her.

Sammy started knocking. "Are you done yet?" he asked.

"I just got in here!" Nina hollered as she kicked off her sneakers.

"Well, I'm going over to the stereo department, okay?"

Sammy said. "At least that way I won't be bored."

"Fine," Nina answered. "I'll be out in a couple of minutes."

She heard Sammy walk away. Then she pulled her sweatshirt off over her head. She couldn't wait to see how she looked in the outfit.

As she was taking it off the hanger, Nina heard something moving around in the dressing room next to hers. "Sammy?" she called out.

There was no answer. But the rustling sound in the next dressing room continued.

"Sammy?" Nina repeated, knocking on the wall.

Sammy didn't answer. A clawing sound did. It was creepy and shrill, like nails scraping down a blackboard.

"Cut it out, Sammy!" Nina demanded. "Stop trying to scare me!"

The clawing got louder and louder.

"You're not even supposed to be in the girls' dressing room, you jerk," Nina scolded.

A high-pitched giggle answered her.

"Very funny," Nina said as she pulled her sweatshirt back on over her head. She was so mad at Sammy, she didn't even want to try on the outfit anymore.

Just then, a dozen pairs of parachute-sized underwear flew over the top of the dressing room wall and landed on Nina's head.

"That's it," Nina hollered, cramming her feet back into her sneakers. "You're dead!"

Nina stormed out of her dressing room and reached

for the door next to hers. "Why do you always have to be such a jerk?" she shouted as she pulled open the door.

But she didn't see Sammy. She saw something else. It was short and green, and all dressed up in a frilly red dress. Its long, twisted toes were crammed into a pair of high heels, and its frizzy red hair stuck straight out of the underwear it wore on its head like a hat. It was standing in front of the mirror putting lipstick all over its face.

Nina let out a scream.

So did the goblin.

"Sammy!" Nina took off running through the store. "There's a goblin in here!"

The goblin took off after her.

"Sammy! Help!" Nina cried. She raced toward the stereo department. But just as she spotted Sammy, she tripped over her untied laces and slid into a stack of speakers.

The little green goblin leaped onto her back.

"Saaaaaaaaaam-meeeeeeeeeee!" Nina wailed. But it was no use. Sammy's ears were buried under a pair of headphones.

The goblin started to yank hard on Nina's necklace.

"Noooooo!" Nina cried. The goblin was trying to strangle her! *"Don't kill me!"*

The little beast pulled Nina's head off the floor by her ponytail. Nina thought it was about to attack her when it ripped off her necklace instead and then jumped off her back.

Nina shot to her feet. She couldn't believe it. The

goblin hadn't been trying to strangle her. It wanted her necklace! Now the creepy little creature was putting it on its own neck.

Nina stood frozen. She wanted her necklace back, but she was afraid the goblin would attack her again.

The goblin didn't attack. Instead it headed toward the perfume counter and started spraying itself with perfume!

Nina ran for Sammy. "There's a goblin in here!" she yelled as she pulled the headphones from his ears.

"Yeah, right," Sammy said.

"There is!" Nina insisted. "Look!"

Sammy's jaw dropped the instant he saw the creepy green blob in the frilly red dress.

"What's it doing with underwear on its head?" Sammy asked.

"Playing dress-up, I think," Nina answered.

"That's definitely not the guy from the tree house," Sammy said. "This one looks like a girl."

"I know," Nina told him.

"Well, she looks pretty harmless," Sammy said.

"Harmless?" Nina cried. "She just stole my necklace!"

"You want me to try to get it back?" Sammy asked.

"No!" Nina told him. "I just want to get out of here!"

Nina and Sammy ran for the exit of Willaby's.

The little goblin didn't even notice. She was too busy loading up a shopping bag with shoes.

"Maybe we should call the police," Nina told Sammy.

"Are you nuts?" Sammy said. "They'll never believe us."

"They will when they see this!" Nina exclaimed. But even she couldn't believe her own eyes. In the mall outside Willaby's were goblins of all different sizes, shapes and colors. They were hanging from balconies and swinging from signs. They were riding on skateboards and boogie boards, bicycles and golf carts. They were playing football and soccer, hockey and darts. Down by the china shop a baseball game was in progress—but the batter wasn't swinging at a ball, he was swinging at vases and plates!

A food fight was going on at the food court. The goblins were eating everything from tacos and pizza to the big giant plants in the big giant pots.

They were sailing in the fountain and dancing on the walls.

Groups of them were racing from store to store loading hundreds of shopping bags and carts with everything they could get their claws on.

Nina thought she was going to faint. The goblins were everywhere. "We have to do something!" she shrieked.

"Like what?" Sammy asked.

"I don't know," Nina cried. "But whenever you stop time, more and more goblins seem to appear. Maybe if we start things up again, they'll all *dis*appear!"

"Good thinking," Sammy said as he reached for his knapsack. "I bet that will . . ." His words trailed off for a second. "Uh-oh," he mumbled. "I don't have my knapsack!"

"What do mean you don't have your knapsack?" Nina said.

"I think I left it in the Ice Cream Palace," he told her.

"Oh, great," Nina moaned. "Now what are we going to do?"

Sammy didn't answer. Just then, the floor started to shake as if an earthquake had hit. But it wasn't an earthquake. It was a goblin—a gigantic purple goblin! And this one wasn't playing games.

It opened its mouth and let out a fearsome roar as it headed right for Sammy and Nina.

CHAPTER 14

Nina didn't move. She stood watching in horror as the enormous creature came closer and closer. His charcoal-gray eyes were fixed on her with a murderous glare. His twelve-inch-long fangs dripped with slimy, thick drool.

Around the warty flesh of his arm was an elastic black band with two red letters that looked like *B.B.* On the top of his head sat a black metal helmet with a six-inch pointed spike.

Nina stood frozen in fear as his long claws reached out, coming closer and closer . . .

"Nina!" Sammy screamed. "Get out of the way!"

Everything around Nina started to get blurry and dark. She felt herself losing consciousness, when suddenly something hit her hard in the stomach.

She went sailing across the floor as Sammy tackled her to the ground to get her away from the goblin's grasp.

"Get up!" Sammy shouted as he pulled her to her feet. "We've got to get to the Ice Cream Palace to get the ball!"

Nina's heart stopped. The Ice Cream Palace was two stores behind the towering purple goblin. There was no way they'd ever get past him!

Sammy knew it too. "Come on," he said, pulling Nina in the opposite direction. "We'll run the other way, around the top floor of the mall."

Nina didn't want to run the "other way." The "other way" was crammed with screaming, football-playing, golf-club swinging, dart-throwing, bunjee-jumping goblins!

"We're never going to make it!" she gasped.

"Just act like you're one of them," Sammy told her. "Maybe they won't notice us."

Sammy started waving his arms above his head like a monkey and gobbling like a goose.

Nina thought he looked more like a slobbering idiot than a goblin, but it seemed to be working. One of the football-playing goblins actually tossed him the ball.

Nina and Sammy gobbled their way past the football players and the golf-club swingers with no problems. But then they reached the dart-throwing goblins.

"Ooch," Sammy yelped as a sharp dart hit him right in the behind. "That creepy little goblin with the mohawk just shot me!"

"Keep running," Nina cried back. Dart after dart whizzed past her head.

Bunjee-jumping goblins crisscrossed their path like miniature Tarzans on ropes. Nina could feel the floor shaking beneath them as the gigantic goblin lumbered after them.

"Hurry!" Nina urged him.

They rounded the escalator and headed back down the other side. As they reached the doors in front of the Ice Cream Palace, Nina heaved a sigh of relief, until she saw what was waiting inside.

The custard machines were pumping like crazy as dozens of goblins in ski caps pumped up mountains of custard to ski on.

There were strawberry hills made of strawberry custard, next to chocolate and vanilla twist peaks that twirled up to the ceiling. Each was capped with gooey hot fudge and sugary sprinkles.

Even the walls in the place were dripping with goo. Snowball fights were going on, with sixty-six different flavors of hard, hand-scooped ice cream!

Sammy's jaw dropped. "These guys really know how to have a good time!"

"Just get your knapsack," Nina commanded. "Now!"

As Sammy slipped and slid his way to the counter, Nina was whacked in the face with a double-dipped chocolate-cookie-dough snowball.

"It's not here!" Sammy cried as he searched the shelves in a panic.

"What do you mean it's not here?" Nina shrieked, wiping the ice cream from her eyes.

Suddenly, the walls around them started to shake. A horrible growl echoed outside the doors. The Goliath goblin was getting closer!

"Maybe they knocked it onto the ground!" Nina shouted.

Sammy leaped onto the counter and dove into a mountain of ice cream.

Just then, the floor beneath Nina's feet started to quake. The thunder of marching feet reverberated throughout the mall. It sounded as if an entire army was about to attack.

And it was.

Two dozen towering purple goblins had lined up behind the giant goblin. Each one was wearing an elastic black armband and a black metal helmet.

"Saaaaaammmmmmmmy!" Nina wailed. "There's an entire army of those big purple guys out here!"

Suddenly, the line of terror started to part. Out from the center stepped a much smaller goblin, just a little taller than Nina. As he took a step forward, the others encircled him as if he were their leader.

One of the goblins inside the Ice Cream Palace let out a shriek—in English! "It's Baldrick!" he screamed. He and the others took cover, diving under the tables and into the ice cream ski slopes. They scrambled to hide in the bathroom and the storage closet. Some of them even climbed up the walls to hide inside the drop ceiling.

Nina wanted to climb the walls too. But instead she

stood frozen, staring at the ominous beast that was glaring at her.

Baldrick's slimy flesh was a deep forest green, and his piercing black eyes practically burned holes through Nina's quivering body. His sharp, pointed ears bulged with pulsating veins that crisscrossed one another like lines on a map. On the top of his head was a row of black scales that ran down his back like a mane.

But the most horrifying thing of all was what came from his mouth.

"Get them!" Baldrick spoke in a deep, evil rasp. "Get them now!"

CHAPTER 15

Nina screamed in terror. As Sammy emerged from the ice cream slope with his knapsack, six of the giant purple goblins lunged toward him. Within seconds, one of the beasts had its five massive claws wrapped around Sammy's neck and was lifting him straight to the ceiling.

"Nina!" Sammy called out. "Help me!"

Nina knew that the only way she could possibly help Sammy, and herself for that matter, was to get her hands on that ball.

Six more goblins stepped up from the line to grab Nina. But she dropped to the floor and crawled quickly through the massive legs that surrounded her.

"Throw me the knapsack!" she shouted to Sammy as she scrambled to her feet.

Sammy tossed the bag quickly. But the knapsack was

open, and as it sailed through the air, the ball fell out and dropped to the floor with a *clang*. Nina gasped as it rolled through the open doors of the Ice Cream Palace and out into the mall.

Nina tried to run after it, but a sharp, pointed claw grabbed the back of her shirt, stopping her dead in her tracks.

She let out a scream.

So did Baldrick. "There it is!" he cried, his eyes flashing like lightning. "The Mystical Orb of Goblinicus! Forget about these humanoid pieces of scum," he ordered his soldiers. "Get me that orb! Once it's back in my hands, you can have all the humans you want!"

"Rib by meaty rib," another voice added. It was the voice of the goblin who was holding Nina. He was glaring straight down at her, licking his lips.

Nina swallowed hard. The hideous fangs looming over her head looked ready to pierce her flesh and chomp down on her bones. But for now Baldrick saved her.

"Move it!" he growled at his followers. "Before one of those lowlifes out there gets his claws on my orb!"

With that, every purple giant in the place took off after the ball, with their grotesque little leader following two steps behind.

Sammy climbed out of the ice cream where his goblin captor had dropped him, gasping, "Those purple guys don't want us. They just want that ball."

"Well, they can't have it!" Nina told him.

"Why?" Sammy asked.

81

"Because if we don't start things up again, we'll never get rid of these goblins!" Nina shouted. "And your mom will be frozen forever!"

At that Sammy turned greener than the goblins. "Come on!" he said, running for the door. "You're right. We have to get it back!"

But that wasn't going to be easy. Out in the mall, the bedlam had turned into a full-blown riot.

The purple giants weren't the only ones after the orb.

Nina watched, terrified, as the golden ball was tossed from one group of goblins to the next, each screaming about finally capturing the "Mystical Orb of Goblinicus."

But no one kept it for long. The giant purple goblins squished, squashed, and smashed every little green goblin that even tried to take the ball.

When the bunjee-jumping goblins took the ball, the purple goblins wrapped bunjee ropes around their necks and pushed them right over the balcony.

When the dart-throwing goblins got the orb, they also got stabbed—with their own pointed darts.

The baseball-playing goblins lost their arms because the purple goblins were ripping them off limb by limb.

"Everybody wants that ball," Sammy gasped, watching the chaos.

But nobody wanted it more than Nina.

She watched as a group of hockey players made a pass for the orb. One by one, the purple goblins crammed the hockey players' sticks down their throats, then broke both the sticks *and* the hockey players right in two. But still the purple giants didn't get the orb. The last hockey player swatted it hard before he swallowed his stick.

Nina couldn't believe her luck. The ball was rolling right toward her . . . but so were a lot of other goblins—on skates.

"Get it!" Sammy cried.

Nina reached down. The ball was just inches away from her fingers. Then before she could grab it, a goblin with a golf club shoved her.

"It's mine!" he cackled as Nina went sailing across the floor on her behind and slammed into the railing of the balcony. "The Mystical Orb of Goblinicus is mine!"

"Correction," Baldrick growled as he lunged for the golf player's throat. "It's mine."

"Never!" the golf-playing goblin proclaimed. He smacked the orb with his club and sent it soaring over the balcony.

Nina's heart dropped to the pit of her stomach as the golden orb fell thirty feet. As it hit the marble landing below, it split right in two.

Nina's heart did the same.

"Sammy!" she cried, staring down at the orb. The two halves were spinning on their sides like a couple of coins. "It's broken! That goblin broke the orb!"

"What do you mean, it's broken?" Sammy yelped, rushing to the balcony to see for himself.

Just then, the two halves spun to a stop. They landed at the twisted-toed foot of a little green goblin Nina was sure she recognized.

"Sammy, look!" She pointed to the creature below. "It's him! It's the goblin from the tree house!"

Sammy recognized him too.

And the goblin recognized them both. "You foolish, foolish creatures," he bellowed as he bent down to pick up the broken orb. "Look what you've done," he said, holding the pieces up for them to see. "Now your world is doomed. Now both our worlds are doomed."

CHAPTER 16

"Illrick, you slimy, slithery little slug," a voice behind Nina shouted. "Bring me that orb!"

Nina spun around to see Baldrick storming toward the balcony. He shoved his way between Nina and Sammy to look over the railing.

"Over my dead body," the goblin below shouted back.

"That can be easily arranged," Baldrick barked.

"What are you going to do, Baldrick, you putrid green pus ball? Sic your morons on me?" The goblin from the tree house laughed as he pointed to the giant purple goblins that were now surrounding the balcony. "Baldrick's Brigade. Now that's a joke. They're nothing but a sorry bunch of giant purple people-eaters who don't know their heads from their own holes in the ground!"

Nina and Sammy exchanged terrified looks. *Purple people-eaters?*

"You know what, Illrick?" Baldrick shot back. "I've waited two thousand years to rip out your heart. If you don't toss me that orb right now, I'll do it with my own claws, right here in the middle of this humanoid marketplace."

"What good will the Mystical Orb of Goblinicus do you now?" the goblin named Illrick replied. He held up the pieces in his claws. "What good will it do any of us? It's broken, you dolt. The ancient powers of the orb are no longer useful to anyone. They're kaput!"

"What do you mean, kaput?" Sammy blurted out in a panic.

"I see that you're as nosy as you are greedy," Illrick answered. "You're lucky I'm not into rubbery flesh or I'd eat you myself! Kaput," he barked again. "It means dead. Defunct. No longer active. You following me now, you stupid boy? In two pieces, the orb has no power at all. Zero. Zip. Zilch. None. Nothing. Nil. It's broken!"

"Is there any way the orb can start time again?" Nina asked, swallowing hard.

"It can't even *tell* time at this point," Illrick growled.

"Shut those two humanoids up already," Baldrick ordered.

"You want me to eat them?" one of the purple people-eaters asked.

"Not yet," Baldrick snapped. "Just shut them up."

Nina let out a whimper as a huge purple arm wrapped around her from behind and covered her mouth with five purple claws.

Sammy let out a muffled scream. One of the giant goblins had covered his mouth too.

"You should be happy now, Baldrick," Illrick called up to him. "Now the surface of the earth is yours, just as you wanted."

"It's not mine," Baldrick barked back. "Not when I have to share it with the lowlifes!"

"No, we don't, boss," the goblin holding Nina chimed in. "All the humans are frozen, except for these two. It's one big picnic up here."

"I'm not talking about the humans, you pod brain," Baldrick said. "I mean the rest of the goblins. Without the orb, there's no way to keep them under control."

"I warned you about this three thousand years ago," Illrick shouted up to the balcony. "But you just wouldn't listen to me, would you? No. You just couldn't keep your grubby claws off my orb."

"*Your* orb!" Baldrick bellowed. "It wasn't *your* orb! It was *our* orb! We were supposed to share it!"

"With everyone," Illrick shot back.

"Spare me," Baldrick spewed. "You just wanted to play Mr. Big Shot. That's all. Mr. All-Important Goblin. Mr. Keeper of the Orb. Mr. Tour Guide at the Temple of Goblinicus. You didn't care about anyone but yourself."

"You're wrong," Illrick said. "And you know it. Everyone was happy back then. Even the humans."

What in the world are they talking about? Nina wondered as she struggled to breathe through the purple claws covering her face.

"Yeah," Baldrick continued. "Well, now *I'm* going to be happy! Because now I'm going to control the power of the orb. All you have to do is fix it."

"That's impossible," Illrick said.

"You're lying!" Baldrick shot back.

"Am not."

"Are too!"

Nina couldn't believe it. The two goblins were arguing like a couple of kids.

"Get him," Baldrick ordered his beasts.

"What about these two?" the goblin holding Nina asked.

"Leave them for now," Baldrick answered. "Without the orb, they're nothing but dinner. Besides, we've stacked up enough frozen meat back home to last a lifetime."

"But the live ones are better," the beast protested. "You get more bloody juice."

"Later!" Baldrick snapped. "Besides, they annoy me! Once Illrick fixes the orb, you and the rest of the Baldrick Brigade can come back out and hunt them down like slugs. Now get him!"

With that, the giant purple goblins leaped over the balcony.

Baldrick himself swooped down like a bat. "One way or another, little brother," he bellowed to Illrick, "you'll fix that orb!"

But Illrick wasn't even looking at Baldrick as the purple people-eaters surrounded him. He was looking straight up at Nina and Sammy with his glowing red eyes.

"You are responsible for this," he growled. "The end of your world is on *your* shoulders."

CHAPTER
17

Sammy and Nina watched helplessly as the purple people-eaters dragged Illrick away. All around them, the goblins who were still in one piece went back to what they'd been doing before—laughing, playing, and looting.

The people in the mall remained frozen like statues. Nina still wasn't sure what the goblins' story was. But as best she could understand, the broken ball somehow determined whether or not the goblins could come up to the surface of the earth. It sounded like Baldrick wanted the orb so that he could control that for himself. But Nina wasn't about to let a bunch of goblins roam loose around her neighborhood and the rest of the world.

"We've got to get that ball back," she told Sammy.

"What's the use?" Sammy moaned. "You heard that

Illrick guy. It's broken. It won't do us any good now anyway."

"Maybe we can fix it," Nina said. "We at least have to try. Come on." She tugged on Sammy's sleeve to get him moving. "We've got to go after those guys."

Nina walked toward the escalator, dragging Sammy along behind her. She picked up speed with every step. "Hurry," she urged him as they started down.

"What about my mom?" Sammy asked, stopping beside his mother halfway down the escalator.

"We're going to have to leave her," Nina told him.

"No way," Sammy said. "I can't just leave her here like this."

"If we don't get that ball back, she may stay that way forever. It's our only hope, Sammy." She waited for him to start moving again.

He didn't. He just stood there looking at his mom. "I'm sorry, Mom," he whispered.

"Sammy, please," Nina begged. "We've got to hurry. We've got to follow them."

"I'll be back, Mom," Sammy said as he got going again. "I promise."

Sammy and Nina raced to the bottom of the escalator and down the corridor to the exit. When they finally burst through the door, they stopped dead in their tracks.

The purple people-eaters were nowhere to be seen.

"Where could they have disappeared to?" Nina asked, looking around the parking lot. "It's like they vanished into thin air."

"Now what do we do?" Sammy wondered.

"I don't know." Nina shrugged.

"Help!" Sammy screamed. "Somebody help us!"

"There is no one to help us!" Nina reminded him. "We're all alone!"

There were people everywhere, but none of them was moving. Time hadn't just stopped inside the mall, it had stopped outside as well. Birds were frozen in flight. Leaves that had fallen off trees hung suspended in midair. The whole world had stopped.

"This is all my fault," Sammy groaned.

It was true. But Nina wasn't mean enough to say it. "This is no time to feel sorry for ourselves," she said, trying to sound braver than she felt. "Let's just try to figure out what to do now."

Nina headed over to a bench beside the mall entrance and plunked herself down on it. Sammy sat next to her.

"Got any bright ideas?" he asked.

Nina stared down at the patch of grass beneath her feet. "No," she admitted.

Just then, Nina heard a noise, a kind of rumbling sound. "Shhh," she said to Sammy, putting a finger to her lips. She listened more closely.

The rumbling was coming from up ahead of them, where a frozen security guard sat on the lawn under a tree about to take a bite of a sandwich.

Nina stood up and took a step toward him. "What's going on?" she asked.

As she took another step, she got her answer.

A hideous green claw popped out of the earth and clamped around one of the guard's ankles.

Nina let out a scream as she jumped back.

A second claw sprang from the dirt and grabbed the guard's other ankle.

In an instant, the man was gone, pulled under the earth. All that was left was the sandwich that had fallen from his hands.

CHAPTER 18

Nina stood staring at the hole in the ground where the security guard had been. "They went back underground!" she yelped. "The goblins went back underground!"

"Oh, man," Sammy cried. "They're dragging their dinner along with them!"

"Get off the grass before they get us!" Nina pulled Sammy onto the sidewalk.

Sammy's eyes were filled with panic. "What are we going to do?" he asked.

"I don't know," Nina answered. "But we have to get out of here!"

"And go where?" Sammy asked. "If the goblins are going under the ground, we'll never find that ball."

"Maybe we should go back to the tree house," Nina

said. "That's where we found the ball in the first place."

"No way!" Sammy protested.

"We have to," Nina insisted. "Don't you remember that Baldrick creep screaming something about the 'Temple of Goblinicus'?"

Sammy nodded.

"Well, maybe that's what they call the tree house," Nina said. "And maybe that's where they took the ball."

"It didn't look like a temple to me," Sammy shot back.

"It's worth a try," Nina urged him.

"And how are we going to get there?" Sammy said. "We're miles away from home. And in case you haven't noticed, there's nobody to drive us."

"We'll just have to walk," Nina said, starting off down the sidewalk. "And stay off the grass."

"Wait a minute," Sammy called out to her.

Nina stopped and turned around. "What?"

"I know how we can get there faster," he told her. "Follow me." He took off running across the parking lot.

Nina tore after him. "Where are you going?" she called as they dashed through a row of parked cars.

Sammy didn't answer. But when he stepped out of the parking lot and headed across the frozen highway, Nina figured it out for herself.

On the other side of the highway was the coolest hangout in the world, even cooler than the mall. So cool that Nina and Sammy weren't allowed to hang out there. Their mothers were too afraid they'd get hurt.

"The Cycle Ranch!" Nina exclaimed.

It was where kids went to ride dirt bikes.

"Good thinking," she said as they raced toward the ranch. "We'll get there much faster on a bike."

"Yeah," Sammy agreed. "And I see just the one I want." He pointed down a hill toward the track.

"Oh, no," Nina said.

But Sammy was off and running again. This time he was running right toward Tony Caputo.

Tony was one of the few kids in town who actually owned his own motor bike. Every day after school he headed straight for the Cycle Ranch. It was one of the things that made him think he was so cool.

Tony was frozen on the first curve on the track. The dirt and gravel his back wheel had kicked up hung in the air.

When Sammy got to Tony, he pulled him off the bike and set him down on the ground.

"Why do you have to take Tony Caputo's bike?" Nina said as she came up beside Sammy.

"That creep has been terrorizing us for years," Sammy answered, climbing on. "Now we have a chance to get back at him."

Nina glanced at Tony's body lying on the ground. He certainly seemed harmless now. But Nina was sure that if they ever managed to start time up again, Tony would get his revenge.

"Come on," Sammy said, revving the bike's engine. "Let's go."

"Do you know how to ride one of these things?" Nina asked nervously.

"It's a piece of cake," Sammy told her. "Climb on." He revved the engine again. This time the bike almost took off by itself. Sammy had to fight to regain control.

"You've never even ridden one before, have you?" Nina took a step back. "Maybe we should just walk." She was convinced that they'd be safer keeping both feet on the ground.

Nina didn't see the claw working its way up through the dirt at her feet.

"Don't be a chicken, Nina," Sammy snapped. "Get on the bike."

Nina shook her head no.

Then she saw Sammy's eyes widen with fear. "Nina!" he screamed. "Look out!"

But it was too late.

The giant purple claw had already closed around her ankle and was tightening its grip!

CHAPTER 19

"Help me!" Nina shrieked. She struggled and kicked, trying desperately to break free of the goblin's grasp.

Sammy dove off the bike onto the dirt near Nina's feet. He grabbed the goblin claw with both hands and tugged with all his might.

The goblin held fast.

Nina couldn't believe what Sammy did next.

He bit the goblin, hard. And he kept right on biting until purple ooze dripped from the claw.

Finally, the goblin released its hold on Nina's ankle. As suddenly as it had appeared, the goblin claw disappeared into the ground.

"Gross!" Nina cried. "That was so disgusting!"

"Let's get out of here fast," Sammy said, springing to

his feet. He kept spitting on the ground as he lunged for the bike.

This time Nina didn't hesitate. "Thanks, Sammy," she hollered as she jumped onto the bike and wrapped her arms around him. "Go!"

Sammy revved the engine, and the bike lurched forward. If Nina hadn't been holding on to Sammy so tightly, she would have been tossed right off the back of the bike.

Sammy zoomed around the track, kicking up dirt and gravel as he headed for the road.

Nina held on for dear life. She wanted to cover her eyes, but there was no way she was going to let go of Sammy. She closed her eyes instead.

When she opened them again, she saw that Sammy was pulling out onto the main road.

Sammy's driving was terrible. If everything else on the road hadn't been perfectly still, they would have been in big, big trouble.

"Look out!" Nina screamed as Sammy nearly plowed into a frozen jogger on the side of the road. They missed him by inches.

A few miles from home, Sammy's driving actually began to improve, especially when they turned onto a straight road. Nina was beginning to believe that they might actually make it to the tree house in one piece.

But before she could relax, they were confronted by another horror. As Nina and Sammy turned into their street, they saw their neighbor, Mrs. Green, standing frozen on her front lawn. Suddenly, a goblin claw reached up and dragged Mrs. Green underground.

"Did you see that?" Nina gasped, pounding Sammy on the back.

Sammy was shaking as he pulled the bike into the driveway and came to a stop. When he turned around to face Nina, she could see the fear in his eyes.

"You don't think the goblins are really eating all these people, do you?" he asked.

"I don't know," Nina answered, looking nervously at the ground around her feet. "I think only the purple ones eat people. Otherwise, those little goblins at the mall would have tried to bite us."

"Then how come it was a green goblin claw that grabbed the security guard outside the mall?" Sammy asked.

Nina shrugged. She didn't have an answer.

"We'd better just stay on the pavement," Sammy said. "I don't think they can reach up through cement."

"We can't stay on the pavement," Nina pointed out. "We have to go into the woods. We have to get to the tree house."

Sammy hesitated. "I guess as long as we keep moving they won't be able to grab us."

"I guess," Nina said. She hoped that was true.

"Ready?" Sammy asked.

"Ready as I'll ever be," Nina told him, tightening her grip around his waist.

He revved the engine and took off again. They left the

blacktop and headed across the back lawn, tearing up grass as they went.

They were almost to the trees at the edge of the woods when Nina screamed. "Stop!"

Sammy put on the brakes. "What is it?" he asked.

"My mom," Nina told him, pointing toward the back of her house.

Nina's mother stood on the patio, her gardening tools in her hands. If she had taken one more step before she'd frozen, she would have been standing on the lawn.

"She'll be okay," Sammy assured Nina. "The goblins can't get her."

"We can't just leave her!" The words slipped out before Nina could think about what she was saying. After all, she'd made Sammy leave his mom at the mall.

"It'll be okay, Nina," Sammy said. "We'll save you, Mrs. Michaels," he yelled. Then he hit the gas and tore into the woods.

Ahead of them, a goblin claw popped out of the ground and made a grab for the front wheel. But Sammy pushed the bike to its limit and sped right over the claw. Nina cringed as she heard the bone-crunching sound beneath them. But she couldn't help feeling triumphant.

"Gotcha!" she exclaimed.

They drove deeper into the woods.

Sammy zigzagged between trees, searching for the Temple of Goblinicus.

Nina couldn't believe that only one day ago she and Sammy had been out in these woods playing, searching for animals. Now her eyes were darting around, searching for something else—something that could determine their very survival.

"Look!" Sammy cried.

Nina looked over his shoulder. She wasn't surprised at the sight of the goblin. That was what she'd expected to see. What she hadn't expected to see was a person.

A shriveled green goblin was pulling a frozen old woman through the woods by her ankle.

"Stop him!" Nina told Sammy.

"I'll run him down," Sammy called out, steering straight for the goblin.

Nina braced herself for a crash.

But there was none.

Just before they reached him, the goblin sank into the ground, dragging the old woman with him.

Sammy swerved, desperately struggling to keep control of the bike.

Suddenly, another claw sprang from the ground. "Watch out!" Nina yelled as the claw grabbed for the front tire.

She heard a loud explosion as the tire popped.

The bike swung to the left, then to the right.

Sammy couldn't hold on to the bike. It flew out from under them and smashed into a tree.

Nina hit the ground hard. Beside her, the dirt began to move. A huge purple claw scratched through the surface of the earth.

CHAPTER 20

"Get up, Nina!" Sammy shouted. He was already standing, frantically watching the ground around them.

Nina scrambled to her feet. A second later two more goblin claws shot up through the ground, right where she'd been sitting.

"We've got to keep moving!" Sammy cried. "It's too dangerous to stay still out here."

They left Tony's bike on the ground and started to run. They'd taken only a couple of steps when Nina spotted the tree house up ahead.

"Look!" she screamed at Sammy.

"I see it," Sammy said.

The two of them took off toward the trees. This time they didn't stop outside the tiny, carved door. They just burst right through it. Whatever dangers might be waiting inside seemed less terrifying than the ones outside.

Sammy was the first one through the door. "There's nobody here," he said, sounding almost disappointed.

Nina looked around for the golden orb. That wasn't there either.

"Now what?" Sammy asked.

One of the long, winding staircases in the center of the room caught Nina's eye. It was the staircase leading down—under the roots of the tree. "We've got to go down these stairs," she told Sammy. "We've got to find out where they lead."

"Are you serious?" Sammy stared at her as if she had lost her mind.

"Of course I'm serious," she snapped. The thought of going underground where the goblins might be didn't make Nina too happy either, but they didn't have a choice. "We've got to find the ball, Sammy," she reminded him.

Sammy walked over to the stairs and looked down into the gaping hole in the ground. "It's pretty dark down there," he said. "Maybe only one of us should go. The other one can stay here."

"Fine," Nina said. "If you're too scared to go, I'll do it by myself."

"I didn't mean that," Sammy said, sounding insulted. "I meant that maybe *I* should go and *you* should stay here."

Now Nina was the one who was insulted. "Why?" she asked. "Don't you think *I'm* brave enough to go down there?"

"Forget it," Sammy said. "We'll both go. But I'm going first." Sammy started down the spiral staircase.

Nina followed him.

At first the stairs seemed perfectly normal. But as Sammy and Nina rounded the first turn, they began to change. Each step was more narrow than the last. Finally they began to feel less like steps and more like the rungs of a rickety old ladder.

"Are you okay?" Sammy asked without turning around.

"So far," Nina told him.

"Hold on tight to the railing," Sammy said. "The footing is getting worse and worse."

So was the visibility. The deeper they went, the dimmer it got. The only light came from above. Below, there was nothing but blackness.

"Uh-oh," Sammy said suddenly.

Nina stopped moving. "What?"

"There's no railing anymore," he told her. "No steps either—just the roots of the tree. You have to turn around and come down backward, as if you were climbing down a ladder. Be very careful," he added.

Nina moved slowly and cautiously. She had to. It was dark and damp down in the hole. And the roots of the tree were slippery with mud.

Nina looked up toward the mouth of the hole. It was no bigger than a tennis ball now. Soon it would be gone completely. Sooner than Nina thought . . .

"Whoa!" Sammy cried a second later.

There was the sound of a scuffle. Then silence.

"Sammy!" Nina called out. "Are you all right?"

There was no answer.

"Sammy?"

The only reply was the echo of her own voice bouncing off the walls of the dank tunnel.

Nina knew that for once, Sammy wasn't fooling around. Adrenaline shot through her. Something had happened to Sammy!

Nina hurried down the roots of the tree, moving faster than she had before.

Suddenly, the root under her foot started to move.

Nina screamed as she slipped and began to slide backward down the root through the tunnel. It was like going down a wavy water slide—but filthy and slimy. And Nina had no idea where it would end.

The light above her became nothing more than a dot. Then it disappeared completely, and Nina was plunged into total darkness, sliding faster and faster.

A second later, Nina's scream was silenced. She hit the bottom hard, and the wind was knocked out of her. She found herself sprawled, face down, in a grimy mud puddle.

"Nina!" Sammy yelled. "Look out!"

Nina lifted her head. Sammy stood in front of her, a terrified expression on his face. His eyes were as big as saucers and fixed on something behind her.

Nina turned her head to see what it was. In an instant, she understood Sammy's fear.

The root she'd been sliding down wasn't a root at all. It was a slug, a gigantic, slimy slug with two huge antennae. The slug slithered toward her, its eel-like mouth open wide enough to swallow her whole.

CHAPTER 21

"Run!" Sammy screamed. In one swift motion, he reached out, grabbed Nina's arm, and pulled her out of the mud.

As Nina took her first step, she slipped and almost lost her footing.

The giant slug inched closer. Its slimy, slithery tongue slapped the back of her neck.

That was enough to propel Nina forward with the speed of a rocket, straight into a tunnel that looked like the belly of a sewer system.

Sammy was running beside her.

Oddly enough, it wasn't dark inside the tunnel. There was an eerie greenish light all around them coming through the cracks in the dank, oozing black walls of the tunnel. The strange light was even brighter up ahead, where Nina could finally see a large opening.

She glanced back over her shoulder. "The slug's gone," she gasped, heaving a sigh of relief. "We don't have to run anymore."

"Where do you suppose we are?" Sammy asked, looking around nervously.

The answer came as they stepped out of the tunnel into a puddle of gunk. An upside-down signpost was hanging in front of them.

Welcome to Goblinicus! it said.

The place smelled like rotten feet.

Nina started to gag. "This is disgusting," she said, waving her hand in front of her face to try to clear the air. But it was no use. The air was so bad in Goblinicus that Nina could actually see a stinky green mist swirling around them.

"Just think," Sammy said, "we've been living right on top of this all our lives and we never knew about it."

Nina wished they'd never found out about it either. But here they were, standing at the edge of an underground city.

It was a terrible city, dismal and dreary. The buildings were little more than lopsided huts. They were packed so tightly together that if one of them fell over, the rest would collapse too, like a row of dominoes.

"Come on," Nina said, dragging Sammy down the muddy road ahead of them. "We've got to find that goblin Baldrick. He's the one who took the ball."

As Nina and Sammy passed between rows and rows of

rundown huts, Nina noticed that there was something odd about their walls. She almost threw up when she realized what it was. "These houses are made out of slug skins!" she told Sammy.

"Gross!" Sammy cringed. He kept his eyes straight ahead to avoid looking for himself.

"I wonder where all the goblins are," Nina said as they continued down the deserted road.

"Maybe they're back up in our world," Sammy suggested.

But Sammy was wrong.

"Did you hear that?" Nina stopped walking to listen. The noise was very faint and far away, but it sounded as if a riot was going on.

Sammy nodded. "What do you think it is?"

"Let's find out," Nina said, heading toward the sound.

Finally they came to a marketplace. It was full of goblins of every size, shape, and color. They were trading things to one another—things taken from the mall.

Nina and Sammy stayed hidden in the shadows of the huts as they surveyed the scene.

"Look," Sammy whispered to Nina, pointing to a little green goblin in a red frilly dress. "There's the goblin we saw in Willaby's Department Store."

"And she's still wearing my necklace!" Nina huffed as she watched the little beast trade a bag full of shoes for a box of chocolates.

But that was nothing compared with what Nina saw next.

At the far end of the marketplace was a stall full of frozen people. Over the stall a big banner had been strung up. It said:

NO MORE SLUG FOOD!
PURPLE PEOPLE-EATERS' BARBECUE TONIGHT!
B.Y.O.P.

"Look!" Nina gasped, pointing it out to Sammy.

"B.Y.O.P.?" he said. "What does that mean?"

Nina knew. She'd seen the letters B.Y.O. on a party invitation once, and her mother had explained what it meant. B.Y.O. stood for *bring your own*. The *P* could only mean one thing. "*Bring your own people*," she told Sammy. "They're going to barbecue people!"

"Let's get out of here!" Sammy started to turn back.

But it was already too late.

"Look!" a voice behind them bellowed. "Live ones!"

CHAPTER 22

Little purple people-eaters appeared as if from nowhere, dozens of them. They were licking their lips and rubbing their claws excitedly as they surrounded Nina and Sammy.

"These two look real tasty," one of them rumbled.

"They'll be great on the barbecue," another growled.

"With extra spicy sauce," yet another goblin added.

There was no place to run, no way to escape. Nina and Sammy were doomed.

"Those two humanoids aren't for eating," a voice boomed in the distance. "Baldrick wants them."

Suddenly, the little purple people-eaters scattered. Nina and Sammy found themselves facing an entire platoon of the big purple people-eaters—Baldrick's Brigade.

"Seize them," the commander ordered.

In an instant, Nina and Sammy were prisoners, thrown into a cage on the back of a rickety old cart.

"Where are you taking us?" Sammy demanded. He tried to sound brave and forceful, but Nina could see his bottom lip quivering.

"Silence," the commander snarled at him. "One more word from either of you and *I'll* eat you for lunch." He abruptly turned away from them. "Back to Baldrick's headquarters," he ordered his troops.

The cart bumped along the pitted, muddy road, pulled by half a dozen henchmen. Nina and Sammy cowered silently in the corners of their cage. Sammy wouldn't even look at Nina. She knew it was because he blamed himself for all the trouble they were in. He knew he never should have taken the ball in the first place.

But right now all Nina could think about was finding a way to get out of this mess. There had to be one.

Unfortunately, she wasn't even close to figuring it out by the time they'd reached their destination.

It was a horrible place, worse than any prison Nina had ever imagined. The building was made of cinderblocks covered with grimy black muck. Huge, slimy slugs slithered up the walls and rested on the roof. Surrounding the building was a thick stone wall crawling with mutated maggots and strange black bugs. On top of the wall were coils of twisted barbed wire. Around the wall was a moat.

The sludge in the moat was thick and green. It bubbled and spit as if it were boiling. Nina was sure there was something alive under all that slime, something that would eat anyone who tried to swim across.

A wooden drawbridge was lowered, and the wheels of the cart clattered over it.

Once they were inside Baldrick's fortress, Nina and Sammy were led from the cart. The commander and several purple people-eaters marched them down a long, dank corridor to Baldrick's office.

The commander knocked on a warped, splintered door.

It opened just a crack, and a red eye peeked out. "I see you've found them," a voice croaked. "Baldrick will be pleased that you've captured them so quickly."

The door was opened by a gnarled little goblin, and Sammy and Nina were pushed inside.

Baldrick was sitting behind a massive, broken-down desk, holding half of the broken orb in each of his green claws. "Fix it," he demanded as Nina and Sammy were brought before him.

"Fix it?" Sammy repeated. "We don't know how."

"Don't lie to me," Baldrick threatened. "Or I'll start ripping your meaty organs out one by one, and I'll set up a smorgasbord right here in my office." The veins in his pointed ears were pulsating with rage. "I need the power of this orb. Illrick said that one of you humans could fix it. Now which one of you can do it?"

"Illrick's a liar," Sammy blurted in a panic.

Nina elbowed him hard in the ribs. "I know how to fix it," she said.

"She does not!" Sammy yelped.

"Yes, I do," Nina insisted, shooting Sammy a look. She wanted to get that orb in her hands. Maybe she could get it back together again, at least long enough to scream "start"—and get them out of there.

"Then do it," Baldrick sneered, holding out the two halves for her to take.

Nina took them in her hands and studied them carefully. The insides of both halves looked like the insides of a space-age computer. There were millions of switches and billions of wires, surrounded by tiny lights that twinkled and blinked.

Nina swallowed hard. She was sure that even a team of rocket scientists couldn't figure out how to put the orb back together again. Still, she was determined to try. With the rounded sides in her palms, Nina began to bring her two hands together, ready to scream "start" the second the halves of the orb touched.

But there seemed to be no way to *get* the two pieces to touch. It was as if each side of the orb was repelling the other, like the same poles of magnets. Every time Nina got the halves within an inch of each other, a force between the two drove Nina's hands apart.

"I'm waiting," Baldrick growled. So did the stomachs of the purple people-eaters beside him.

Nina couldn't panic. "Just give me a minute," she said, hoping that she would get lucky this time. She switched the piece in her right hand with the piece in her left, praying that somehow that would make a difference. It didn't.

"What do you know about the Mystical Orb of Goblinicus?" Baldrick asked Sammy as Nina continued to work.

"Just that it stops time," Sammy said.

Baldrick chuckled. It was a deep, evil sound. "Yes," he said. "Stopping the human world was the best thing you could have done for me. Now goblins will rule the earth. And of course *I* will rule the goblins—once your little friend fixes that orb."

But the orb wasn't getting fixed. It wasn't even coming together, no matter how hard Nina tried.

Baldrick's short fuse finally ran out. "You two humans are worthless," he bellowed, snatching the halves from Nina's hands. "Illrick *is* a liar. Take them to the hole," he told his guards. "And make sure you don't bruise them too badly. I'm going to want them later—for dinner."

CHAPTER 23

Baldrick's men dragged Nina and Sammy out of the office and down to the "hole."

"Welcome to your new home," one of them sneered as he lifted what looked like the lid to a sewer. Then he raised Nina from the ground and tossed her into the hole.

Nina screamed as she fell. She couldn't tell how deep the hole was, but she seemed to be falling a long way. Finally, she hit the ground and toppled over into the soft, gooey mud that made up the floor.

Sammy came flying after her. He landed with a sickening *thud* and collapsed to the ground in a heap.

Nina got just a quick glimpse of the place before the lid slammed shut. The only light came from a tiny hole in the center of the lid. Nina couldn't see more than a few inches in front of her.

It didn't matter really. Nina didn't have to see the prison to know how bad it was. The smell told her everything she needed to know. Compared with the hole, the rest of Goblinicus smelled like a beautiful spring day.

"Sammy?" Nina choked.

"Yeah?" he groaned.

She was about to ask him if he was okay, but she stopped herself. It was a stupid question. Sammy was not okay. Neither was she. They were in a mud hole, in the pit of the earth, with no hope of escape.

"This is all my fault," Sammy sighed.

Nina knew that Sammy never meant for any of this to happen. She wished that she could think of something to say to make him feel better. But words failed her. So she reached out and touched Sammy's hand instead.

"If only I hadn't taken that orb . . ." His voice trailed off. "I promise," he started again, "if we ever get out of here alive, I will never touch anything that doesn't belong to me, ever again."

If we ever get out! If! Nina tried to push the thought out of her head. They *had* to get out. She couldn't spend the rest of her life in a dark, smelly hole. Or let herself get roasted by a bunch of purple people-eaters.

We will get out of here, she told herself. *Somehow we'll . . .*

Nina's moment of bravery was shattered when she heard a rustling sound.

"Sammy," Nina gulped.

"What?" he asked.

She didn't answer. She was busy listening.

"What is it?" he said impatiently.

She heard it again.

"I don't think we're alone," she whispered. "Listen."

The sound was still there, more insistent now. They were definitely not alone. Something was in there with them, moving around in the darkness.

CHAPTER 24

Nina began to scream. She was sure that the creature stepping out of the shadows was there to start carving them up.

The dim light moved across the creature's arms, then up to its warty green shoulders. Its sharp, pointed claws were already touching the side of Nina's throat.

"Noooooooooo!" Nina cried in a panic. "I don't want to be a goblin's dinner!"

"Then you'd better shut up and listen to me," a familiar voice answered her back.

Nina's breath caught as the creature's face came into view. It was Illrick. Around his neck was a collar with spikes. But the spikes weren't sticking out, they were sticking in, right through his flesh. Globby green ooze trickled out from his throat and dripped down his chest.

His ankles were chained together. And he was missing some of the claws on his twisted-toed feet.

"What happened to you?" Sammy gasped.

"Baldrick," Illrick answered. "Every time I lie to him, he sends one of his morons down here to chop off a toe. They ought to be back any minute for another. That stupid, putrid pus ball thinks he can get me to fix the orb by torturing me. But the only thing he's doing is making me more irritated."

"You're irritated with Baldrick?" Nina asked nervously.

"No, not with him," Illrick growled back. "I've had two thousand years to get over my irritation with him. It's you two who have my blood boiling now. In fact, I ought to chop off *your* toes for putting me in this position in the first place."

Nina quickly curled her toes away from the tips of her sneakers as she took a step back from Illrick.

Sammy took two steps back. "Why are you mad at us?"

Even Nina shot Sammy a dirty look as Illrick's flashing red eyes bugged out of his head farther than they already were.

"Would you like a list?" Illrick growled. "If you want, I can carve it into your flesh so that you're constantly reminded of what a disaster you've caused!"

Sammy started to open his mouth to say something, something that was bound to be stupid. Nina quickly backhanded Sammy in the gut and spoke up herself.

"Listen," she said, trying to keep Illrick calm. "We're really sorry that we took the orb from you in the first place. But we had no idea that anything bad was going to happen. We thought the orb was like a Lava lamp ball and that you were just a statue."

"A Lava lamp ball?" Illrick was getting more irritated anyway. "That's what you thought the Mystical Orb of Goblinicus was? A Lava lamp ball?"

Sammy nodded sheepishly.

"I've dissected thousands of human brains in my lifetime," Illrick huffed, "and I still can't figure out what makes you people so stupid. The Mystical Orb of Goblinicus is all-powerful. It is the force that maintains the balance of the earth, above and below. As long as it was resting in the Temple of Goblinicus, the creatures under the earth were able to coexist peacefully with the creatures on the earth."

"What's this Temple of Goblinicus?" Sammy asked. "Your tree house?"

"Did that tree look like a temple to you?" Illrick snapped.

Sammy shook his head. "I told you." He snapped, too— at Nina.

"Read my lips, kid," Illrick barked. "I'm only going to tell you this once. Thousands of years ago, when our parents expired, Baldrick and I were appointed Keepers of the Orb and Guardians of the Temple of Goblinicus. Back in those days, goblins were free to enjoy the riches on the earth as well as below. We could come and go as we pleased, as long as the orb stayed in the temple, which stood in the center of Goblinicus. Then Baldrick came up with a cunning plan."

"To steal the orb," Nina said.

"Right," Illrick answered. "He wanted the two of us to have total control. When he stole the orb, the temple collapsed. And so did Goblinicus. While Baldrick lived the high life, using the orb to have everything he'd ever wanted, the rest of Goblinicus went to pot. Every goblin in earth had to rely on Baldrick for food, shelter—everything."

"But you're his brother," Sammy said. "Didn't you get to live the high life too?"

"For a brief time," Illrick answered. "Until I recognized that Baldrick's ways were destroying our city. So I stole the orb back from him and took it to the tree house, sealing off Goblinicus forever. Without access to the top of the earth, Baldrick had nothing. The best part was that Baldrick didn't think I would do it."

"Why not?" Nina asked.

"Because ancient law dictates that any goblin who brings the orb to the surface of the earth turns to stone. This prevents him from using the orb's powers against the human race," Illrick answered.

"Wow," Sammy said. "So you became a statue to help the other goblins?"

"Until you came along," Illrick growled. "Once you took the orb from my claws, the power was in your hands. The gates of Goblinicus opened wide, and all the goblins who had been cooped up down here were released. It's no wonder they're completely out of control. The top of the earth is a lot nicer than this dump!"

"Can't you fix the orb?" Nina asked. "Baldrick thinks you can."

"Baldrick's an idiot," Illrick shot back. "Besides, even if I knew how to do it, I wouldn't tell him. The stakes are way too high now."

"What do you mean?" Sammy asked.

"Well, now that the orb is broken in two, there's only one way to piece it together again. . . ." Illrick's words trailed off for a second before he continued.

"To reattach the two halves of the orb, the hand of a goblin and the hand of a human must come together. Otherwise, the halves will repel each other. But when they do come together, only one world will survive. The other will be sealed off for good. And all its inhabitants will turn to stone."

"Do you know which world will be destroyed?" Nina asked nervously.

Illrick shook his head.

Nina felt as though she'd been punched in the stomach. This was not the news she was hoping to hear. Fixing the orb could turn out to be even worse than leaving it broken.

CHAPTER 25

"It's toe-chopping time, Illrick," Baldrick's voice boomed above them. Light filled the hole as one of Baldrick's thugs lifted the manhole cover on the sewer-like prison.

Illrick squinted to see. "Which one do you want?" He laughed, lifting the foot with three twisted toes left.

Nina cowered against the gritty dirt walls, hoping it wasn't also dinnertime. Sammy huddled beside her.

"You have one last chance to tell me how to fix this orb," Baldrick bellowed. "Or I'll start cutting off more than your toes!"

Nina didn't know what she was hoping for now. If Illrick spilled his guts and the orb was fixed, she and Sammy and the rest of their world might turn to stone. But if they didn't take that chance, she and Sammy would definitely end up on the barbecue, and the rest of the human world would be frozen anyway.

"What's it going to be?" Baldrick snarled.

"Chop away," Illrick answered. "I'd rather be a dead goblin than one that has to suck up to you!"

"Bring him up," Baldrick ordered his thugs as he spat in disgust. "And while you're at it," he added, "bring up my dinner as well."

Three long metal rods dropped into the hole from above. At the end of each was a sharp rounded hook. Holding the poles were three giant purple people-eaters with helmets and armbands.

Nina let out a shriek as one of the hooks caught Illrick's spiked collar and lifted him straight out of the hole.

"How are they going to hook on to us?" Sammy yelped, dodging the rods as the purple people-eaters fished for their food.

Nina was thinking exactly the same thing. And something told her that the purple people-eaters weren't going to try to hook *on* to them at all. They were going to drive their hooks right through them!

"Grab hold of that rod and let them pull us up," Nina told Sammy. "Before we get stabbed."

"Are you nuts?" Sammy shot back. "Either way, they're going to rip us wide open!"

"Just do it," Nina ordered, grabbing hold of one of the hooks herself.

As Nina gave the rod a tug, she was lifted off the ground.

Sammy quickly grabbed the other rod. Within seconds, they were being lifted through the hole, side by side.

As Nina was dropped into the filth at Baldrick's feet, she did the only thing that offered any hope at all. "I know how to fix the orb!" she cried, looking up into Baldrick's gruesome face.

"You do not," Baldrick grumbled.

"I do too," Nina insisted. "Illrick told me how!"

With that, Baldrick's pointed ears perked up even higher than they already were.

"She's lying," Illrick roared, shooting Nina a furious look.

"She *is* lying," Sammy chimed in as he scrambled to his feet.

"I am not!" Nina shouted.

"Don't do this, Nina," Sammy pleaded. "There has to be some other way."

"There isn't," Nina said. "We don't have a choice."

Baldrick's eyes narrowed as they darted back and forth between Nina and Sammy. "Can you fix it or not?" he demanded.

Nina gagged as his hot, stinking breath slapped her right in the face. For a second, she couldn't even speak. She nodded instead.

"Then do it!" Baldrick held out the two halves of the orb. "But I warn you," he threatened, "if you don't get it right on the first try, you'll be missing your liver before you can even think about trying again."

"I can't do it by myself." Nina choked out the words. "You have to help me. We each have to hold one half."

"Don't do it," Sammy pleaded with Nina.

"Shut up," Baldrick snapped. "This had better work," he said to Nina as he handed her one half of the orb.

"Tell me about it," Sammy mumbled under his breath.

Nina inspected her half of the orb. She turned it over and over, looking for some way to tell which half she held—the safe half or the half that would turn her and every other person on earth into stone.

There was nothing that gave her a clue.

"Put them together already!" Baldrick commanded.

Suddenly, Nina had a bad feeling about her half. "Wait," she said. "This is the wrong half. I have the goblin half."

Baldrick impatiently switched halves.

As soon as the other half touched Nina's fingertips, a tingling sensation crawled up her arm.

"I'm sorry." She stopped Baldrick from putting the halves together again. "I was wrong. We had it right the first time." She exchanged halves before Baldrick had a chance to protest.

"Are we ready now?" he growled.

The answer was no. Nina wasn't ready. She would never be ready.

What if the tingling half was the safe half?

Something was wrong. The halves did not fit together easily as Nina imagined they would. In fact, they were still pushing apart. Maybe Illrick was lying again. Maybe he just liked torturing *everybody*.

Nina put all her weight into pushing her half against Baldrick's.

There was a loud *pop* as the force field between the two halves exploded.

Nina felt a jolt of electricity run up her arm. She grew dizzy. The dirt walls around her started to spin.

The orb was whole again.

But Nina didn't know that. Because she was suddenly enveloped in darkness.

CHAPTER 26

"Nina!" Sammy cried.

His voice sounded strange, as if it were coming to her from far, far away.

"Nina!" he cried again.

Nina couldn't see him. She couldn't see anything. She was trapped in darkness.

She tried to move. She couldn't.

No! she thought to herself. *No!* She and Sammy were turning to stone. She was sure of it.

"Ni-na!" Sammy's voice was more insistent. Someone was shaking her.

"Sammy," she managed to mumble, surprised her lips could still move. Her eyes fluttered open.

Sammy was kneeling beside her, looking down at her with a worried expression. But he definitely wasn't stone!

"Thank goodness," he sighed. "You're all right."

"What happened?" Nina asked. She tried to raise her head off the dirt floor, but it was too heavy.

"You fainted," Sammy told her. "And you missed the whole thing. Look," he said, lifting her up into a sitting position. "We're surrounded by stone!"

Nina couldn't believe her eyes. Towering over her were dozens of goblin statues. Baldrick, Illrick, and the purple people-eater brigade were harmless now, and as hard as rock.

"What about the orb?" Nina asked.

"It's in Baldrick's hands!" Sammy laughed. "Just the way he wanted it, back in one piece."

Nina scrambled to her feet. "What about us?" She was starting to panic again.

"What do you mean?" Sammy asked, confused. "We're fine."

"I mean, how do we get out of here?" Nina yelped. "Illrick said that Goblinicus would be sealed off from the earth for good. Don't you remember? What if we're sealed up in Goblinicus too?"

Sammy's look of triumph quickly melted away. "Come on," he said, pulling Nina by the hand. "We've got to get outside and see what's going on. Maybe we can get all the people together and climb up the roots of that tree again."

Nina and Sammy took off through the winding dirt tunnels. Luckily, it wasn't long before they found their way back up to the first floor of Baldrick's fortress.

Upstairs, every goblin in sight had turned to stone.

They raced through the huge, warped doors at the building's front entrance, but they weren't at all prepared for what they saw when they stepped outside.

Above them, the surface of the earth was opening into giant-sized pores. Stone goblins were dropping down all around them.

"The earth is sucking all the goblins back in!" Sammy cried, as he and Nina swerved out of the way of the falling stone goblins.

"Let's just hope it lets me and you out," Nina shouted as they ran across the rickety drawbridge.

The moment they hit the center of Goblinicus, they were confronted by an even more amazing sight. One by one, the people who were supposed to be the main course at the barbecue were getting pulled up to the surface of the earth. Swirling green mists swept out of the ground and carried them through the air like rockets.

"Everyone really is going to be okay!" Nina exclaimed.

"Yeah," Sammy said. "Everyone but you and me."

Nina's heart sank. It looked like Sammy was right. No swirling mist was carrying them back home.

Within seconds, Goblinicus was totally cleared of humans—all but two.

Maybe Illrick left this part out, Nina thought. *Maybe whoever was responsible for taking the orb in the first place ends up being doomed anyway.*

No! Nina refused to allow herself to believe that. "Come on." She pulled Sammy along. "We have to find that tree again. Maybe we can only get out of Goblinicus the way we got in."

Sammy's expression showed that he didn't believe that for a second. But he didn't say a word. What could he say? It was their only hope.

Nina and Sammy ran and ran until they finally found the tunnel that led to the roots of the tree. Nina hoped that the giant slug wasn't waiting at the entrance.

It was. But it too had turned to stone.

"Hurry," Nina said, climbing the slug's marble-like back.

Sammy climbed up behind her.

The opening in the tree root seemed to be getting smaller and smaller.

Nina took hold of the inside walls of the root, then pulled herself through, with Sammy clinging to her ankle.

The moment they were inside, the root sealed up behind them.

There was nothing to do now but climb in total darkness. As they climbed, even though it was getting harder and harder to breathe, Nina tried to assure herself that they wouldn't end up suffocated in a tree root.

Finally, she felt wood beneath her fingers, wood that felt like the rungs of the ladder at the bottom of the staircase.

"Sammy!" she exclaimed. "We're almost at the staircase!"

Then Nina saw light coming from above. She practically flew up the rest of the tree.

"We did it!" Sammy shouted as they reached the tree house. "We made it alive!"

As the words left Sammy's mouth, the staircase under their feet collapsed and crumbled into the ground. The gaping hole that remained in its place was sealed up a moment later by shale and stone that closed over the top of it like two elevator doors sliding shut.

The ball game was finally over.

CHAPTER 27

Nina and Sammy hurried out of the tree house door.

"What do you think we should do about this place?" Sammy asked, looking over his shoulder.

"We should come back and board it up," Nina answered. "Nobody should ever come in here again."

A shudder went through her. Goblinicus had been destroyed forever. But Nina would never forget those horrible goblins, or that disgusting hole where Baldrick had dropped them.

"Listen," Sammy said suddenly.

Nina smiled. "Birds!" she said happily.

All around them, birds were singing. The world was alive again.

"Come on, Sammy," she said. "Let's go check on our moms!"

But Sammy just stood there for a minute. Nina could tell he was still thinking about the goblins too. "It's all over, Nina," he said. "The goblins are gone." He smiled nervously. "You know what? For a little while, I really believed our livers were going to be flame-broiled like a couple of—"

Suddenly, a ferocious growl cut him off. "You two are dead meat," a voice snarled.

Sammy saw who it was before Nina did. "Tony Caputo," he gasped. "What's he doing here?"

Tony Caputo stepped out from between the trees, and Nina saw that he was dragging his battered bike.

"I knew it was the two of you," Tony growled as he approached. "I don't know how you stole my bike right out from under me, but I was sure it was you. And when I came to your houses, I saw the tracks in Nina's backyard and followed them into the woods. And here you are. You're both gonna pay for this." Tony dropped the bike onto the ground now and continued toward them, his hands balled into fists.

"Tony," Sammy said, holding his hands up in surrender. "You don't understand. You've got to let us explain."

Tony didn't stop until he was nose to nose with Sammy. His hands were still in fists, but they hung at his sides. "You've got one minute," he said. "Then I'm gonna pulverize you. First for ruining my bike. And second for getting me in trouble on the bus and in the classroom. I don't know how you pulled that off either. But I'm sure it was you."

"We can explain," Sammy said, backing away.

Tony moved right along with him.

Nina stepped in between them. She figured that Tony would be less likely to beat her up. "Tony, this is going to be really hard to believe," Nina warned him. "But—"

"Then I don't even want to hear it," he butted in. He tried to push past Nina to get at Sammy again.

Nina held her ground. "Tony, you've got to listen. See that tree over there?" She pointed to the goblin's tree house. But before she could continue, Tony got away from her.

He headed for the tree house. "What is this? A little club house?" He laughed at the two of them as he reached for the doorknob.

"Don't go in there." Sammy tried to stop him.

But Tony shook Sammy off easily and stepped inside. Nina and Sammy followed him.

"Cool!" Tony exclaimed, looking around.

"It's not cool," Nina told him. "This is a goblin's house."

"Yeah, right." Tony laughed at her. He walked over to the shelf that held the eggs. "And I suppose these are all the eggs the goblin laid." He reached out for the biggest one.

"Don't touch that," Sammy hollered.

He'd hollered so loud that he startled Tony. The football-size egg almost tumbled from Tony's hands. But Tony recovered his grip on it in the nick of time.

Unfortunately, in the process, he bumped into the shelf hard enough to knock it off the wall.

Egg after egg crashed to the floor.

"No!" Nina screamed. "No!"

But it was already too late.

One by one, the shells cracked open, giving birth to dozens of purple people-eaters. And before anyone could make a move to stop them, they skittered across the floor and out the door, and disappeared into the woods.

Get ready for more . . .

Here's a preview of the next spine-chilling book

from A. G. Cascone.

LITTLE MAGIC SHOP OF HORRORS

Peter and his friend Bo need an act for the school's talent show. An ad in the phone book leads them to a strange little magic shop . . . and an act that's sure to knock 'em dead.

The shop looming in front of them looked as if it had been closed for a hundred years. The front window was covered with so much grime, Peter couldn't see inside.

But it was definitely the right place. It said so on the window, in bright red letters that looked as if they'd been written in dripping blood.

THE LITTLE MAGIC SHOP OF HORRORS!

"Do you really want to go in there?" Bo sounded unsure.

"Are you kidding?" Peter said. "This is going to be great."

When he pulled open the door and stepped through, a tinny-sounding bell jingled overhead. He looked up at it as Bo followed him inside.

The store appeared to be deserted. In fact, it looked as though no one had been inside the place in years. Everything was buried under inches of dust, including the floor. Peter and Bo left footprints as they walked.

"Hello," Peter called out nervously. "Is anybody here?"

There was no answer.

"Maybe we should leave," Bo suggested.

"No way," Peter told him. "Not until we have a look around. There's a lot of cool stuff in here. Check this out." Peter pointed to a life-size skeleton standing behind the door.

"Gross!" Bo cried. "He's got eyeballs."

"That's what makes him so cool." Peter laughed. He walked closer to the skeleton to get a better look.

As Peter moved, so did the skeleton's eyeballs. They seemed to be following him. "Neat trick," Peter said. "I wonder how it works."

"There are probably batteries in there that make the eyes move around," Bo said.

Peter supposed that was right. Still, it was pretty eerie the way the eyes seemed to follow his every move. Peter stared up at the skeleton for a couple of seconds before turning his attention to other things in the store.

"Look at this." He headed over to a black box that was almost as big as a phone booth.

"What's that?" Bo asked, coming up beside Peter.

"I'll bet it's a disappearing box," Peter told him, opening the door.

"How do you suppose it works?" Bo asked.

"I think there's a secret compartment behind one of the walls," Peter answered. "When the magician closes the door, the person in the box hides in the secret compartment. Then, when the magician opens the box again, the person inside seems to have disappeared."

"It doesn't look like there's anyplace to hide inside this box," Bo said as he examined the walls.

Peter felt around for himself. Bo was right. The walls were pretty solid. It didn't look as though there was a secret compartment.

But there had to be. It was the only way the trick could work.

"Maybe the door has to be closed before the secret compartment will open," Peter speculated. "Go inside and try," he told Bo.

"Are you nuts?" Bo shook his head. "I'm not letting you close me in that box. *You* do it."

Peter didn't like the idea of being shut inside a dark box either. But it would be worth it if he could make himself disappear—just to scare Bo.

"Fine." He stepped into the box. "Close the door and count to twenty."

Confident that the secret compartment would be at the back of the box, Peter faced the back wall as Bo closed the door.

Peter was surprised at how dark it got. It was pitch black. He closed his eyes tight to block out the darkness. Then he began feeling around for the secret compartment.

He could hear Bo counting outside the box. "Four . . . five . . . six . . ."

Peter pushed against the back wall hard. "Come on," he said. But the wall wouldn't give.

Maybe it was one of the side walls. Peter slid his hand along the back wall until he got to a corner and turned to face the side wall.

"Eleven . . . twelve . . . thirteen . . ." Bo kept right on counting.

It was useless. The side wall wasn't budging either. But Peter wasn't about to give up yet. There was one last wall to try and not much time.

He turned around to face the other side wall. He took a step forward, reaching his hands out in front of him, his eyes still closed.

He was surprised when he didn't feel the wall—so surprised that he opened his eyes. It didn't help; it was still pitch black.

He stretched his arms out farther as he took another step. No wall . . . but—

A scream exploded from Peter's throat.

Something was in the box with him—and it was alive!

About the Author

A. G. Cascone is the pseudonym of two authors. Between them, they have written six previous books, two horror movie screenplays, and several pop songs, including one top-ten hit.

If you want to find out more about DEADTIME STORIES or A. G. Cascone, look on the World Wide Web at:
    http://www.bookwire.com/titles/deadtime/

Also, we'd love to hear from you! You can write to
    A. G. Cascone
    c/o Troll
    100 Corporate Drive
    Mahwah, NJ 07430

Or you can send e-mail directly to:
    agcascone@bookwire.com

Read all of the silly, spooky, cool, and creepy